T0277368

Also by Yuri Herrera

SEASON OF THE SWA

SEASON OF THE SWAMP

A Novel

YURI HERRERA

Translated from the Spanish by Lisa Dillman

Graywolf Press

Part of this novel was written with support from the Awards to Louisiana Artists and Scholars.

Published by Graywolf Press
212 Third Avenue North, Suite 485
Minneapolis, Minnesota 55401

www.graywolfpress.org

Published in the United States of America
Printed in Canada

ISBN 978-1-64445-307-0 (cloth)
ISBN 978-1-64445-308-7 (ebook)

2 4 6 8 9 7 5 3 1
First Graywolf Printing, 2024

Library of Congress Cataloging-in-Publication Data

Names: Herrera, Yuri, 1970– author. | Dillman, Lisa, translator.
Title: Season of the swamp : a novel / Yuri Herrera ; translated from the Spanish by Lisa Dillman.
Other titles: Estacíon del pantano. English
Description: Minneapolis, Minnesota : Graywolf Press, 2024.
Indentifiers: LCCN 2024011418 (print) | LCCN 2024011419 (ebook) | ISBN 9781644453070 (hardcover) | ISBN 9781644453087 (epub)
Subjects: LCSH: Juárez, Benito, 1806–1872—Fiction. | Juárez, Benito, 1806–1872—Exile—Louisiana—New Orleans—Fiction. | New Orleans (La.)—History—19th century—Fiction. | LCGFT: Biographical fiction. | Alternative histories (Fiction) | Novels.
Classification: LCC PQ7298.418.E7986 E8813 2024 (print) | LCC PQ7298.418.E7986 (ebook) | DDC 863/.7—dc23/eng/20240313
LC record available at https://lccn.loc.gov/2024011418
LC ebook record available at https://lccn.loc.gov/2024011419

Jacket design: Carlos Esparza

Jacket art: North Wind Picture Archives / Alamy Stock Photo

1853. Benito Juárez has served as judge, deputy, and governor of the state of Oaxaca. But he has yet to become the man who will lead his country's liberal reform, first as minister and then as president, and he is certainly not the hardheaded visionary who will lead the resistance against France's invasion of Mexico and restore the republic. Nevertheless, he's managed to make a number of enemies, in particular Santa Anna, who will not forgive Juárez for forbidding his entry into Oaxaca in 1847, when Santa Anna fled the capital after the disastrous war with the gringos. This is why now, back in power, Santa Anna has Juárez arrested and sent into exile.

In his autobiography, Apuntes para mis hijos (Notes for my children), Juárez describes in detail his arrest, the long journey to San Juan de Ulúa prison, and his exile to Europe via Havana, where he decides to stay and plan his return. Here, his account becomes terse. He says only:

In Havana "I remained until 18 December, when I left for New Orleans, where I arrived on the 29th day of that month.

"I lived in that city until 20 June 1855, when I headed to Acapulco to lend my services to the campaign . . ."

Juárez says not a word about his nearly eighteen months in New Orleans, not a single one, despite the fact that while living there he met up with other exiles, despite the fact that it is there that he evolved into the liberal leader who would transform the trajectory of his country over the decades to come. Apart from two or three vague anecdotes that appear in the multiple biographies of Juárez, no one knows what happened in New Orleans.

It is this interval, this gap, in which the following story, or history, takes place. All the information about the city, the markets that sold human beings, as well as those that sold food, the crimes committed daily and the fires set weekly, can be corroborated by historical documents. The true account of what happened, this one, cannot.

For Tori

SEASON OF THE SWAMP

ONE

The badges dragged the man from the ship, hurled him down the gangplank, and he fell in front of them and then attempted to stand, but the badges conquered him with clubs and he didn't defend himself from their blows, because his hands were clasping a treasured object to his chest. One of the badges torturing him said Drop it. They didn't speak the language, but that's what the badge was saying. Drop it! shouted the one who seemed to be the boss, and then he insulted the man; they didn't recognize the word but they recognized the language of hate. But the man did not drop it, not until three badges wrenched one arm and three wrenched the other, and the object fell to the ground and popped open, and the boss picked it up, and though he'd no doubt held objects like this one before, he was astonished to see that it was a compass.

In that frozen moment in which the badges looked at the boss and the boss looked at the compass and the man looked at the boss holding the compass and nobody knew what to do, he caught a glimpse of the tattoo on the man's back, on his shoulder blade, a glyph of a bird walking one way while looking the other.

Then time unfroze, the boss snapped the compass shut,

turned, and walked off, and his badges lifted the man up only to drag him off like a beast once more and disappear into the throng.

Then everything kicked into action: the cranes hoisting sailboats, the ships loaded with hay and coal, the cotton—so much cotton, hundreds and hundreds and hundreds of bales of cotton—the mountains of produce being unloaded, the smell of fresh produce, the smell of rotting produce, the promiscuity of incomprehensible voices, the people bustling here and there, the smell of the people bustling here and there; to the left, dark water specked with lights; ahead, the dim lights of lampposts; to the right, the twinkling lights of the city.

They let themselves lurch between the stevedores and the men who suddenly began to swarm them, offering things and pointing this way and that.

He leaned over to Pepe and shouted into his ear did he have the address. Pepe looked stricken. What was it, what was it. A hotel. Mata had sent word that he'd wait for them at a hotel. A hotel named for a city. Or a state. Or was it a person. Something with a C.

"Hotel Chicago?" he shouted into Pepe's ear.

Pepe made squint eyes.

"Hotel Cleveland?"

Pepe dubitated, not dissenting, just dubitating.

"Hotel Cincinnati?" he asked.

Though the voices around them were a sea of unnavigable sounds, one of the squawkers accosting them beamed and, face aglow, said:

"Hotel Cincinnati," and tapped his own chest. "Hotel Cincinnati."

Then gestured for them to follow.

He shrugged and said to Pepe Let's go, and the city sucked them up like a sponge.

The man walked fast but kept turning back to ensure that he and Pepe were following; after climbing down from the levee and entering the actual city-city—less congested but more mud— their guide began to walk slower and slower, until he stopped entirely, then whistled in no apparent direction, and from the alley emerged a little kid to whom he gave instructions using the universal sign for writing, and the kid took off running. Their guide turned back to them and thumbs-upped in triumph, then walked on once more.

They came to a house with a torch over the door. With a majestic flourish, their guide, spent, offered them the narrow square door as if it were the entrance to a palace. Beside it, a strip of cloth read Hotel Cincinnati.

They entered single file; inside, the boy was still holding a hammer in one hand and a strip of fabric in the other; behind him was a dark hallway, a rocker, a fireplace around which were arranged several armchairs where three sailors sat warming their hands, and an oak table where an austere woman sat, already asking Yeah, what? with her nose.

He pulled out the documents he'd shown at customs, but the woman shook an impatient head and thumbed her fingertips in the universal sign of This is what I'm talking about. So he pulled out some of the money he'd brought, in pesos, which the woman assessed for a moment before she nodded, They're legit, took them, and gave an order to the kid, who trotted off down the hall.

They followed him to an inner courtyard containing nothing but broken chair parts and stacked-up tables, and a door at the back, which the kid opened for them. Two cots. One whole chair. A hook to hang clothes on. A pewter basin. The kid pointed to another door on another side of the patio, with any luck the toilet. The boy gazed at them in silence for a minute. Then made the universal sign of Welcome to the Hotel Cincinnati and left.

His reception on disembarking from the packet boat had been a foretaste of all that was to come: waiting and waiting and not knowing words and not being seen and learning the secret names of things.

When it was finally his turn he had pulled out his papers, but instead of taking them, the bureaucrat supposedly helping him had asked a question or two: Where are you from? Why have you come? What do you do? What is your name? Not all of them: one or two. He decided to reply to them all, one by one. The official gave him an exasperated look, snatched his papers, and began copying down his details, but when he reached Occupation the bureaucrat stopped and asked him something. Looking at the word the bureaucrat pointed to, he replied Abogado, lawyer. The bureaucrat gazed at him blankly and wrote Merchant, and then paused again on seeing the age listed on the document: 47. Looking up, the man studied him in genuine curiosity, almost amiably, and wrote 21. The bureaucrat also wrote the wrong date of arrival, though perhaps

6

it wasn't the bureaucrat but he who was wrong: for a long time now he'd had no idea what day it was.

He'd kept his mouth shut when his papers were handed back. And Pepe had been dispatched much quicker.

They had been on their way out when the compass man landed at their feet.

A cockroach traversed the ceiling as if setting out across the desert, illuminated by a band of light coming in from the courtyard. They tracked its progress in silence even though each of them knew the other was awake. They watched it wander back and forth for a while. Then Pepe said:

"When can we go back?"

The cockroach turned and scuttled off to a corner.

"Soon, no doubt."

They had to find the others. The next morning, he inquired as to whether Mata too was lodging there, writing out Mata's name and mimicking the man's long mustache. Mata was not lodging there. He asked more for the sake of it than out of any actual optimism. By this point he suspected that if the Hotel Cincinnati even existed, this was not it. But there was no point asking for the real Hotel Cincinnati, as if they might reply, Oh, you wanted the *real* Hotel Cincinnati.

They drank a hot drink aspiring to tea, which the austere owner logged in her little notebook, then put on their coats and set out. For a few minutes, they stood on the sidewalk in silence.

Though it was a sunny day, the street failed to register this fact. It wasn't the worst cold he'd ever felt, but it was a slow cold that, rather than strike all at once, took its time finding just the place to let a layer of frost slip in under his coat. They walked to the corner and looked in every direction. No sign of yesterday's crowds. They headed for the river, and as they neared it, the streets perked up: there came a smell of burning coal, shops began to open here and there, they heard whistling. A drunk, wakening to the horrific news that he was no longer drunk, looked their way with the clear intention of asking for alms, but quickly changed his mind.

Arriving at the levee, they headed to the spot where the compass man had been hurled. Somehow, he had hoped for a sign of what had happened, any sign of the beating, of the adrenaline, of the onlookers. There was nothing.

Back at the grand Hotel Cincinnati, they walked in to find two sailors bumping chests and chins right there in the, uh, lobby. The sailors spat saliva, tobacco, and insults like dogs separated by a fence, or perhaps not separated, since one leaned over all casual-like and took down the poker hanging beside the chimney, while the other—surprisingly agile, given all that hair, all that flesh, all that rum on his breath—took a step back and pulled from his armpit or who knows where a fat rope with a heavy ball on one end; he swung it around once, tracing a perfect circle, as though to furl the heat from in front of the fireplace, and the second time around he cracked the other sailor's skull.

It was a beautifully fluid moment, despite the appalling sound the sailor's skull made as it split. He and Pepe would come to find that such juxtapositions were quite common here.

The austere innkeeper snapped her fingers and signaled to the kid, who tugged down his cap, put on his coat, and ran off, while the husband—the one who'd guided them to the world-famous Hotel Cincinnati—pulled a pistol from under his armchair but didn't point it at the sailor, who, though no longer swinging his weapon, was still brandishing it, bent arm aloft; the husband simply offered a couple of calm suggestions: time to stand back, put down the weapon, don't be a jackass, one or two of those.

The sailor rolled up his weapon and tucked it back under his arm, his calm methodry in stark contrast to his endless shouting. Then the loud and living sailor bent over the collapsed one, opened his coat, and from an unusually broad pocket pulled out a pair of pants. *His* pants. The husband followed all this with interest but not judgment, pistol in hand, a simple fact, nothing more. Slowly, the sailor grew calm and began making comments about the man whose blood and cranial matter were now splattered about the room: that's a shame, he was asking for it, I didn't mean to, one or two of those.

After a few minutes the badges arrived, all slack-like, as if they'd just been dragged from a toasty-toes bath. Three of them. One sent another to examine the victim while he questioned the victimizer, who explained with his hands, mouth, pants, and weapon what he'd already said. The officer asked for the sailor's weapon by name: slungshot. It was only then that *he* was actually able to appreciate the object. A round, heavy, ball-like mass at one end, covered in thin ropey fabric; the fabric was stained with blood, and not all of it was fresh: ochre specks dotted its entire circumference.

The interrogator wore an understanding expression while attending to the tale, nodding along, and seemed to side with the aggressor, tsking his head back and forth to signal What an outrage, for one man to lay a hand on another's property. He gestured to the third officer, who wasn't doing anything, that the man should be taken in; officer three unhitched from his pants a pair of exceedingly heavy cuffs, but officer one signaled that the cuffs weren't necessary, and then turned to number two, who was attempting to find the victim's pulse, and shook his head; the order-giver gave the order to haul off the corpse but showed no sign of lending his own hands, instead rubbing them together in the universal sign of Mission Accomplished, and then turned. The innkeeper's husband took pity and helped officer three drag the victim away. A moment later, the austere innkeeper began mopping up the sanguineous intimacies smeared all over the floor.

Given that he and Pepe were witnesses, he assumed they'd be interrogated, but the officers didn't so much as glance their way. Or rather: they glanced their way for a second, without registering them as anything other than wallpaper.

For two days they took turns guarding their meager possessions: clothes and pesos—few and suspect—a book from Havana about the United States Constitution, letters from Margarita, a few documents. One of them would go sit by the fire for a spell while the other kept watch inside the room. Who was to say thieves wouldn't be back to strike the magnificent Hotel Cincinnati once more.

On their second day he found a newspaper. Unintelligible at first sight. Like when he'd taught high school physics and his students stared at the symbols and formulas on the chalkboard as if they were all just some kind of inhuman scrawl. Then he'd explain how each number and each symbol *did* something when joined together, and how the something that they did was in fact profoundly human, and his students began to glimpse a new world in those equations, the same way you see animals in the clouds, except these animals actually existed.

A few words he knew, others he intuited. He spent that second day carrying the paper back and forth between guard posts without anyone demanding it back. He was able to decipher ships' schedules and cargos; ads for dance academies and moving companies and guesthouses (they already had a place to stay, though, at the Cincinnati, no less); news of a woman—"a lover of the arts," the article called her—who had stolen a statue from someone's house; a story about a Spanish ballerina, "Señorita Soto," who'd performed several numbers never before seen outside of Spain; the arrest of a man accused of obtaining money under false pretenses (how elegant it sounded); several carriage drivers detained for furious driving (so beautifully put); a woman who had stabbed her husband; an article about Sonora, noting that it was a very rich state and that soon an expedition from California would set out to quash the Apaches (to steal Sonora, more like it, though that's not what it said); cures for gonorrhea; rewards for runaway slaves; and an advertisement that destroyed him, for a Slave Warehouse. The ad was accompanied by a wee little drawing of a man who was supposed to be a slave, with a bundle tied to a stick over one shoulder, as if he were traveling—as if the man were doing the one thing it was utterly impossible for him to do. His eyes remained fixed on the image like it was the longest article in the paper.

"All that, in a place you could cover with a gob of spit. Unbelievable, isn't it?"

Someone had spoken behind him. In Spanish. He turned his head to see a thin balding man, wrapped in a coat meant for bigger bones. There were bags of honest exhaustion beneath his eyes and he had very fine hands, like a boy.

"Rafael Cabañas," he said, holding out a hand.

He held out his own hand and offered his name in return.

"Is this paper yours?"

"And yours; give it back whenever you're done."

Cabañas sat down on the opposite side of the fireplace.

"What brings you to the city?"

He heard an affectation in Cabañas's cee and suspected the man would have high-flown zees and vees as well.

"A slight diversion, a delta, you might say."

"This whole city is a delta, so you've come to the right place."

"Not for us." He pointed to Pepe, who had just arrived for the changing of the guard. "Pepe Maza, my brother-in-law. We're only here for a few days. As soon as we find our compadres, we'll be off."

Cabañas laughed.

"If you knew how many people have only been here for a few days, for years."

He chose not to respond to this.

Cabañas broke the uncomfortable silence.

"So where are your compadres?"

Now Pepe was the one to laugh.

"Not at the Hotel Cincinnati."

"At a hotel that starts with a cee."

"With a *thee*, with a *thee*," Cabañas thetaed loftily. "None come to mind just now. Have you looked for it?"

12

"We tried, but after what happened," he said, indicating the stain left by the sailor's shattered skull, "we decided to stick close to our things."

"Good thinking: these rooms have a way of disappearing possessions, like magic." Cabañas glanced at the inkeeper's husband, dozing in his rocker. "I'm surprised they were able to pull one over on those two. But you can't sit here forever. Let me make you a proposition: my printshop is a few blocks away; you can leave your valuables there."

From the corners of their eyes, he and Pepe exchanged the universal look of mistrust.

"Or not. As you wish. But who knows who might carry off your cases here; at my place at least you'd know the thief was me."

He looked over at Pepe once more, they nodded.

Then he handed Cabañas back his paper.

"Till tomorrow, then," said Cabañas.

"Where are you from?" he asked as he headed off to his room.

"Méjico," Cabañas replied, and though it sounded just the same as when he said it himself, he knew Cabañas had said it not with a Mexican ex but a Spaniard's jay.

"First, coffee."

Cabañas had knocked on their door early and they'd had to gather their things quickly, as if making an escape.

"On me," he added, sensing their hesitation.

They walked back toward the levee once again, but this time down streets on which they hadn't ventured.

"This is the *vege*table market," Cabañas veed iberically.

13

The joyful ruckus reminded him of the markets of Oaxaca: the haggling, the passageways, the clinking spoons, the moist-earth smell; yet the shouting here had its own cadence, the vegetables came in other shades, their green seeming to spill over the tables, and also there were coffee stalls on wooden carts. Cabañas chose one that read Café de Thisbee and began extolling the beans they used. But he paid no attention to Cabañas, paying it instead to the exchange Thisbee was having with another vendor. What were they saying? And what were they saying it *in*? He knew how to read French, and though he couldn't speak it, he'd often heard it spoken by people returning from Europe who talked about Europe all day and occasionally brought an actual European back with them, and if said European was French, then the climber in question insisted they demonstrate, so as to impress the audience, who was nearly always impressed. But what he was hearing now was not French. It sounded like French, but kind of *bettered* somehow, as if it had been unhitched from the dictionary and gone out for a stroll. The two women seemed to be discussing a transaction, shouting gleefully, Ah, non, non, no way was I going to pay him for that crap, Course you weren't, Does it look like I was born yesterday? You were definitely not born yesterday, sister, You either, Me either, something along those lines. Thisbee suddenly fixed her gaze on him and said, most likely, What're you looking at?, but then smiled and went on talking to her friend.

She was very beautiful, her blackness a shade he'd never before seen, curls piled high like a tower on her head and her dress layered in color.

"Try others if you like, but I'll save you the time: this is the most interesting coffee in the city," Cabañas pontificated. "Right, time to go."

His printshop was on the other side of the quadrant, or quarter, which they called the old quadrant, but in French, le vieux carré, the old square, la vieja plaza—old quadrant was better; many of the streets and buildings had French names even though the architecture looked just like what he'd seen in Havana.

Cabañas loaned them a box for their things, which he stuck behind another box, which he stored under a table to make them feel safer. Then, as Cabañas prepared for work, he and Pepe nosed around the printshop, looking at the machinery, the movable type (please don't touch, Cabañas said when Pepe picked up some letters from an already-assembled text), the variety of paper, the posters and pamphlets all ready to be delivered. Among them he saw a poster offering a reward for a fugitive.

"Doesn't it bother you to print this sort of thing?"

Cabañas seemed confused by the question.

"Ads for the capture of enslaved people."

"Well, I'm merely the printer, and that's the law, it's not like anyone's capturing them in order to take away their freedom. They never had it to begin with. Officially, there's no more importing of slaves, so with very few exceptions, they were born into it."

"They were still captured," he said. "Worse: captured by birth."

Cabañas cocked a brow as if something had gone click, though more out of curiosity than indignation.

"I suppose you're right, but that doesn't change anything; the only way they can truly be free is if their owner files a load of paperwork and puts down a deposit that isn't returned until it's proven that the freedman has left Louisiana. Pff, theoretically not only left Louisiana but gone to Africa, though generally speaking no longer being here is sufficient."

Truly. *Truly* be free, if their owner so decides. Are the ones who are in fact freer not those who ask no permission? But he didn't say that, he said this:

"But I know there are people called freedmen of color."

"Ah, well, you see, their parents or grandparents were free, having bought their freedom—which you can't do anymore, officially, though it's still done—or the owner freed them for some reason—out of gratitude or spite, as a way not to bequeath them to their own families and an attempt to screw them over—but even then they have to go through a whole to-do. Or they could be the children of a woman the owner freed. But it's certainly not common: you should see how many men are happier to be owners than parents."

He decided to make the most of Cabañas's tutorial.

"What about the creoles? Are they the same as our criollos? Europeans born here?"

"Ah, the creoles." Cabañas joined thumb and index finger and made as if to whip out an invisible handkerchief. "Ooh-la-la, les creoles. It's quite complicated. Being creole is, in a manner of speaking, a presumptuous way of saying: I'm from Here, truly-truly-truly from Here. But even that can mean different things. You've got your small-c creoles and your capital-C Creoles. The capital C is reserved for whites who were born here and have French ancestors, the kind that founded the city; then also aspiring to the big C are those who aren't white-white but whitewashed and boast about being

16

white—though when they're with other whitewashed they boast about the color in their blood, the color of those who fled Haiti before it was called Haiti, for example. The small c is for those who were born here, and that's enough for them to say they're creoles, though there are also some who you can see their color but they dress and speak and trade like whites and think that's enough to wash them white. And plenty of them speak Creole, which is . . . how can I put it? Like French but kind of *bettered* somehow."

Of course! He nodded.

"So being creole isn't a fixed thing, then."

Cabañas shrugged.

"It's quite complicated. If you want to be on the safe side, just remember that on one side are the whites, and on the other everyone else. There might be whites living in poverty, but so long as they're white they can marry, own property, file lawsuits, et cetera; and then there's everybody else, who can't do any of those things, or they can but with restrictions. Freed people of color, say, can sell fruit but not alcohol, and they can go to the theater. Slaves can do only those things that are permitted by their owners. Even among slaves there are distinctions: there are plantation slaves, who go out only on Sundays, and city slaves, who are still slaves but sometimes live independently, though they're required to hand over any money they earn from other work to their owners, who then give back a portion of it."

He turned back to work and said for the last time:

"It's quite complicated."

Though they'd been in the city several days, it wasn't until the next one that they noticed the reek of shit in the morning.

The second they walked out of the Hotel Cincinnati they were assaulted by the penetrating stench of fresh shit, exposed to the elements; only then did they see what passed for a sewage system here: open gutters along which waste flowed al fresco.

They wrinkled their noses—what can you do?—and walked on. After a few steps, he said to Pepe:

"Let's get coffee first."

The stall that Cabañas had recommended was packed. Thisbee was ladling coffee from a huge pot, scooping it up with one cup and pouring it into another, splashing customers as well as her own hands, but nobody complained; she gave each customer their coffee and a command, Move it, mostly likely, because the people paid and then moved down a bit to drink it; with one hand she took their money and with the other she picked up the next mug. Suddenly she saw them and smiled like they were acquainted.

Pepe brought him a coffee from another stand. They stood drinking in silence, watching people make commerce. As they headed out, he turned to see if Thisbee would smile at him again. She didn't, but he saw something, or thought he did. He couldn't be certain, though, for he was starting to discover that he needed a new language to understand what he saw as much as what he heard: on Thisbee's arm was a tattoo, same as the one he'd seen before.

They zigzagged through the old quadrant, passed a theater with opera—Opera, he said, Verdi's *Jerusalem*—a daguerreo-type business, a lot of places called coffeeshops where a lot of people were drunk, hungry dogs—one, two, three, four, five, six, ten, twenty, so many dogs—a fabric shop, a courthouse—mental note: courthouse—a social club. Finally they came to the edge of the old quadrant, crossed over to the other side, passed a square where a military contingent was practicing formations, and kept walking. Now it was not so much city-city as its spillover: there was more and more wild oak, more and more swamp. And though there were still houses, the only businesses were carpenters', coffeeshops full of drunks, and cabarets—Cabarets, Pepe said. The houses were less solid, seemed softer, like the ground, and they began to see swarms of mosquitoes and different animals, not just mules and horses and dogs but iguanas, possums—Possums, said Pepe—and a snake.

It smelled different too, this was a defiant smell, water and detritus. The vegetation and the water and the snake were suddenly all defiant; and it was beautiful here, and it wasn't.

"We better go back," he said.

Back at the hotel they saw that the rag strip at the entry now read Hotel Saint Charles.

"Isn't the Saint Charles the most expensive hotel in the city?"

"Not anymore," said Cabañas. "Apparently now it's this dump, which is quite cheap; that's why I live here."

"So what's the actual name of this dump, then?"

"Well, for the time being it's the Saint Charles, until the folks at the Saint Charles find out. Normally it doesn't have a name: that was for your benefit. But people are going around saying there are thieves at the Cincinnati, so the Hotel Cincinnati no longer exists."

And the Cincinnati had been so distinguished! Alas. Good times.

Later, Cabañas told them the best way to the lake, which

was out where they'd been headed without realizing it. There was a road, Esplanade, that went direct, without going through the swamp. Cabañas also said:

"By the way, if either of you needs work, I need an assistant—but only one."

They nodded without giving it much thought. After all, they'd soon be on their way, so what difference did it make.

Cabañas left them that day's paper and then took leave himself.

The paper reported that a group of Protestants had put up flyers criticizing the Catholic bishop; that one captured man had been arrested for stealing a pair of shoes, another for stealing bread, yet another for biting an officer; that a woman had been taken in for dressing in men's clothing, as had two men just before fighting a duel—a duel? give me a break—and three musicians for playing harps and violins without a license.

And finally they found the others. Like so many things that would accidentally befall them, it only happened because this was a city that served up accidents on a platter. A carriage hurtled toward them as if the driver and horses were fleeing a fire, he and Pepe threw themselves against a wall, the carriage drove past furiously, mere centimeters away, Pepe followed it for who knows what reason, and then on reaching the corner he stopped and stood pointing at something on the other side of the street.

"Conti," Pepe said to him, as soon as he had caught up. "Hotel Conti."

That was the C. The C of the deeply incognito Hotel Conti. They walked in and asked for Mata. The receptionist gave them a look that said he might end up sullied merely by laying eyes on them. The man searched for the name—Mata, Mata— found it, gave them the room number, and indicated the way, as well as a little mat on which they should wipe their feet.

The second Mata opened the door, Pepe embraced him with outsize joy, especially since the two were not close; he himself threw his arms around Ocampo, who'd just arrived with his daughter Josefa and was a man he knew by deed but not in person; Arriaga he did know, and not only did they embrace but actually said to one another Benito; Ponciano; So glad you made it, Benito; We've been looking for you for a week, Ponciano, though it wasn't true: they'd been agonizing for a week, with no clue how they were going to find them, but looking-looking, no.

"Let's go down to the restaurant and have some coffee," Mata said. "The Conti has an excellent restaurant."

He opened his mouth but said nothing, unwilling to speak of penury a second after they'd found each other—after all, they were lodging at the Saint Charles. But Ocampo must have seen the words leave his mouth without his having to say them, because he declared:

"My treat."

They all remarked on the same things, in scorn and won- der: there are drunks everywhere, and it's impossible to get anywhere without ending up covered in mud, and the drivers all drive so furiously, and it reeks, it reeks, it reeks, and if this is winter, imagine what it's like in summer, and sometimes you hear music but have no idea where it's coming from, and how ironic it is to be exiled by a tyrant, only to end up in a city full of captured humans ("slaves" is what they said), and the houses are so beautiful, and the levee's a miracle, and there's so much commerce, it's like a small country with all the commerce here, all the freedom here. Silence fell after those last words, a sort of unspoken shame at all their enthusiasm. Then Mata said:

"We must call a meeting."

They already were meeting, of course, but Mata meant a Meeting with a capital M, one in which all would become solemn and historical, in which the participants—not *him*, for he made a conscious effort not to—would suddenly begin speaking as if Andrés Bello's *Indications on the Benefit of Simplifying and Normalizing Orthography in America* had been implanted into their mouths or as if they'd been seized by the spirit of Simón Rodríguez.

They scheduled the Meeting for the following day, right there at the Hotel Conti. The others suggested meeting up at the Saint Charles, but Pepe told them not to bother: it wasn't actually as nice as everyone said.

It was only after the coffees were in hand that Pepe pointed out the obvious.

"We just had coffee."

And they hadn't eaten.

"And we haven't eaten," he added.

"Let's see if we can find something around here. Unless you'd prefer to keep eating the hotel's skin-and-bone broth. Nothing we might find could be fouler, and it might actually be cheaper."

This was true, though they'd come not for the coffee but for Thisbee, the only person to have smiled at them since their arrival. He hadn't intended to speak to her, just wanted to be near her. But she understood some of what they were saying and gestured with one hand.

Eat must be what she said. You two want to eat?

They nodded. With her fingers, Thisbee said, Right, then show me what you got; he pulled out a coin; she shouted to a girl at a fruit stand and then told them to follow.

Thisbee took them to a house outside the old quadrant, in a direction they'd yet to venture, with less blanquitude, more brunitude, and endless untroubled oaks just oaking around, as if, hands in pockets, they were merely watching folks go by. The house was made of ship-wood—thick planks, hardy, some still encrusted with barnacles—and had one door at the front and another at the back, aligned for airflow.

They sat at a long bench at a long table while Thisbee served them two bowls of a thick, steamy soup that smelled of seafood, of celery, of onion, of spice.

"Gumbo," she said.

Normally they would have hesitated, but there was something about the consistency and aroma of the stew that made them snatch up their spoons and attack, not stopping till they'd scraped bottom, and then they proceeded to rip apart the crayfish in the bowl to suck on. Thisbee laughed and remarked on how fast they ate.

Then she said Come, opened a door, and showed them a room no less shabby than the one at the Saint Charles but larger and with a window that looked out on an oak tree. She held up eight fingers, pointing to the room and the dining room.

"Well?"

"Allow us to discuss it and we'll let you know tomorrow,"

he said in what was evidently not the universal sign for tomorrow, because Thisbee mimicked it, uncomprehending; in her hands the gesture looked like a little hill in the air.

He was about to try to explain a different way, but she made a face like Ah, gotcha, mañana, mañana, and then: Mañana, she said in Spanish.

They set out to explore their surroundings. He still didn't know what he was seeing. Since they'd arrived, the landscape had been dotted with phosphenes, like when you shut your eyes tight. He knew what he needed to do to see better.

"Take my arm," he said to Pepe, "and walk slowly."

He closed his eyes. Listened. A rooster, a chicken, a dog, the distant hammering of metal, a horse pulling a carriage (without fury), birds flitting after each other before going to sleep, his own footsteps on the muddy road, children shouting, laughing, squealing. He opened his eyes.

They stood before an enormous house with a number of outbuildings. An old sign said Olivier's Plantation; a newer one, St. Mary's Orphan Asylum. In a flash he saw them both in the same place, like a series of daguerreotypes in a flipbook, violently changing while remaining the same.

"Which places are SAFE, where can we return to?" asked Arriaga.

The Hotel Conti's restaurant, which he'd paid no attention to on his first visit, because of the phosphenes, resembled some sort of pre-Jacobin holdout right there in the swamp: golden armchairs, golden curtains with golden ties, floor-to-ceiling mirrors, porcelain tableware, captured waiters in white gloves.

"**Epitacio Huerta** is in Michoacán," said Ocampo.

"**Vidaurri's** in **Coahuila**," said Mata.

"Oh, & **Álvarez** is in **Guerrero**," said Arriaga, "all though Álvarez is a mystery."

"Álvarez is no mystery," he said, "Álvarez is against the tyrant, there's no doubt about that; Epitacio Huerta, I'm not sure; but the problem is Vidaurri, he's no mystery: Vidaurri is a scoundrel."

"We can deal with **Vidaurri**; I mean, the man won't walk a step without a huarache—he's out for his own—but we hand him one his size & it's a done deal."

"Then we go to **Brownsville**," said Mata, "& from there to **Coahuila**, & from **Coahuila** some of us can head to **Michoacán**"— and here he pointed to Ocampo—"and others to **Oaxaca**"—and here he pointed to him—"while the rest of us seek refuge in **the Capital**."

It sounded like a solid plan until Pepe, who was at the meeting without being at the Meeting, for though technically also exiled, he wasn't one of the Exiles, said:

"So our plan is to hide?"

No one said a word. Instead, they sipped coffee, as though that might expunge Pepe's question.

"We're already in hiding," Pepe continued, "and at least here nobody wants to kill us."

No one said he was right, precisely because they all knew he was, but that fact wasn't a very Historical one. They continued sipping their coffee.

"We send **letters**," Mata finally said, "we sound out Vidaurri, firm things up with **Epitacio Huerta** & with **Álvarez**."

"Álvarez is already two steps ahead of us," he said. "Álvarez doesn't need us. Yet."

This time they were vocal in their assent.

"Let's send **Comonfort**," said Arriaga, "to sound him out. In person. That way we'll already have a presence in Guerrero if the revolt takes off."

"But what's the *plan*?" he asked. "What is it that we want to go back *for*?"

"The plan we put together on the fly," said Ocampo. "First we must WIN THE WAR."

"First we must *start* the war," said Mata.

"The country's always at war," he said. "What do we want to do after we win, is what I'm asking. The revolutionary thing would be to try to avoid war."

Everyone gawped at him but Pepe, whose eyes were on a creole señorita.

"However much or little we do, & I sincerely hope that it's *much*," said Ocampo, "it won't get done by sitting around staring. We're not mannequins."

"We're not marionettes," said Arriaga.

"It's imperative that we set THE REVOLT in motion; once it gets going, we can give it direction. And if, as you say, **Álvarez** is already halfway there, we won't be starting from scratch."

He wanted to say that *he* was in a hurry to get home too, but they couldn't proceed blindly, they needed a plan. But their minds were made up.

"So we agree to send *letters* to **Huerta** & **Vidaurri** & send **Comonfort** to Guerrero?" asked Mata.

They all said yes and immediately the mood changed. They agreed to have Mata and Ocampo write the letters and to have Arriaga send word to Comonfort.

"Now we await *good tidings*," Mata said.

Wait, no two ways about it. Wait, and not go back. For who knows how long. Doing who knows what.

The minute he left the hotel he foresaw, with terrible clarity, the prospect of mediocrity and monotony on the horizon. His family back there, sad and stricken. The country held hostage by a one-legged madman, deluded he was emperor. And all of them there, waiting. He'd melt on the spot, in the cold, of preemptive tedium, be reduced out of sheer boredom to bones, to dust, to nothing.

This was not the isle of Elba and they were not heroes: they were pariahs, freeloaders.

Just then, a few blocks away, something burst into flame like an enormous match, and a man walked by singing a song.

TWO

The most pivotal thing to happen in the weeks that followed was the drumming; no, the most pivotal thing in the weeks that followed was the dances; no, the most pivotal thing in the weeks that followed was the concerts; no, in a way it was kind of the hippodrome, which was fun and also pivotal though in another way; no, the most pivotal thing to happen in the weeks that followed was the inner courtyard, yes, that might be it; or maybe the most pivotal thing to happen in the weeks that followed was that he met the canaille and learned what funk was; or that he more or less figured out what Thisbee might or might not have done. What happened in the weeks that followed was that they stopped feeling like weeks and instead sometimes felt like minutes, and the minutes sometimes felt like days, because the city—first gradually, then vertiginously—stopped being a city of cons and wheeling and dealing and became a living creature, an animal that initially began to wriggle and writhe as if shaking off sleep or fleas and then as if nothing in the world mattered more than dancing.

Even the sailors had their own music, and not just inner music, not just the singsong bitch and moan all down the street by

29

the levee, singsong bitch and moan about making no money—
money was one word he did know, a key word if ever there
was—and about other things he didn't understand; at the
front, a fiddler and a man with a military drum that he beat
with military talent, bom-bom, bom-buh-bom, rhythmic and
energetic, while the fiddler played dance tunes, quick and
peppy, that nobody danced to, since they were all walking,
everyone but him, who accompanied the fiddle by nodding in
time to the melody as if there were dancing couples doing little
leaps and turns inside it.

On and on they walked, and saw the Théâtre d'Orléans,
which was staging a production of Meyerbeer's *Robert le
diable*, a very old opera, as well as *Le prophète* (*Le prophète!*),
which had premiered in Paris only four years ago, so basically
yesterday. What a place, forever renewing itself as though the
swamp made no matter.

The streets were perpetually under construction. Now that
he and Pepe were staying at the boat-house in the third ward,
he could walk to work, traversing the old quadrant to get to the
printshop. He'd learn to sidestep the holes on one street and
then find the next day that workers were patching it, only for
it to begin crumbling again, then be patched again, over and
over. The streets were under slapdash repair more often than
they were traversable. Occasionally the workers would rush
around, portraits of exemplarity; more often they'd sit on the
sidewalk to smoke, drink, and sing. There was a lot of singing.

Cabañas wouldn't let him touch the movable type. His job
was to stack the ads or notices or pamphlets or invitations and
deliver them. On rare occasion he was tipped a coin for his
trouble, but basically he had to make do with what Cabañas

paid him; in exchange, between trips through the quadrant (most deliveries went either there or to the anglo ward, on the other side of Canal) and reading the paper at the printshop, he started to see that despite the cold, the city was hotting up.

"Carnival," Cabañas said. "It's like everybody gets an itch that can only be scratched by going nuts."

He saw a man steal a dog—steal a dog, when there were already so many on the street—and watched the owner catch and beat the thief with the metal handle of his cane while the dog did its part by ripping the man's leg to shreds. He read of a woman arrested for stealing two corsets. Corsets. A city where there were battles over corsets. He saw two men challenge each other to a duel and a third befriend them both with a bottle of rum. He read of a man called to court to explain what a captured man who didn't belong to him was doing at his house. He saw a lost child and did not approach.

One day, returning to the house-boat, he heard drums. This wasn't the little military drummedy-drum drumming of the singsong sailor, the bom-bom, bom-buh-bom, but more of a *baaam*-bam-bam-bam, *baaam*-bam-bam-bam, like that; he didn't know this language either, but it was clear that somebody was making the most of those drums, playing them like keyboards, a hypnotic *baaam*-bam-bam-bam, but a *baaam* that was also changing its attitude, like when you truly communicate something instead of just say it.

He stood awhile at a vague crossroads (street demarcations in this part of the city were still more suggestion than law), trying to locate the source of this percussion. *Baaam*-bam-bam-bam. It sounded close but also like it was in many places, all around.

31

He entered Thisbee's house, distracted by the rhythm in his head, without thinking, without knocking. Thisbee was in her room, sitting on a bed, holding hands with another woman. She turned, on hearing him come in. For one second her eyes flickered in apprehension, the next second they narrowed in anger, and the second after that she stood and closed the door.

They lost both their money and each other, on account of following parades: some small, others that started small but were teeming a few blocks later; one led them to the place they saw their first fire—a shop on the edge of the old quadrant—which took no time to engulf the two, three, four, seven houses around it; in Spanish, someone said, Folks want to burn their own damn house, fine, everybody's got to get their gravy somehow, but leave the neighbors out of it. The parade hardly paused, the band—fiddles and flutes and a drum—was backlit by the flames and continued to play in the light provided by three captured, holding torches aloft; from time to time something would rain down on them, oil or some other fuel, who knows, liquid fire, but the captured did not complain.

Another parade led them to Saint Louis Cemetery; they accompanied Ocampo and Arriaga to that one. Arriaga told him that someone at the Conti said this was the place for visitors but he didn't see why:

"They look just like the ones in Mexico, though there's more graves aboveground than beneath, true."

Later he learned why.

"What you may not have heard," said Ocampo, "was that the man said this is where visitors come *to stay*, and then he said Wait till summer."

The parade after that was the one that led them, all five of them, to the hippodrome. It was an afternoon parade, with a band playing on a float, and several masked men, the first masks they'd seen: birds, reptiles, fantastical animals.

Immediately on entering the hippodrome they separated. The place was like its own sort of river, one where luck was the only deal being done. They saw whites, whitewashed, and creoles of color, of varying degrees of elegance. Those who looked the poorest were also the most hopeful, like at church; the richest bet in an offhand manner, as though fanning themselves.

He watched the races for a while, less interested in the results than in the muddy clop-clop of the horses, until he saw Pepe gripping one of the railings that bordered the track, slips of paper in hand. No, no, no, no, no.

He approached him and made the gesture of Say it isn't so.

"Two times, only twice, and I almost won, it was so close, I mean, closer than close," said Pepe, adding, with great conviction: "but look who's running in the next one, look who I bet on!"

Pepe held out the racing form. He'd already seen them back at the printshop, they looked to him like poems, the horses' names listed one after the other. He looked where Pepe was pointing triumphantly: La Mejicana. That was the horse's name, spelled with an imperial jay.

Pepe signaled Eh, eh, eh? How could I not?

It was a single lap. La Mejicana, svelte and sorrel, was number two. The horses shot out of the gates and immediately La Mejicana pulled ahead, as did ten, an enormous graceless beast but one with a gallop full of fury. He heard himself urging on two before becoming conscious of the fact that he was shouting like a fool Go, two, go, two, go, go, goooo, and yet he didn't care, just as in the days to come none of them much cared about any kind of foolishness. La Mejicana was snorting, and ten, blasted ten, was snorting, and the other horses eyed their competition from afar. Screw you, losers, Pepe screamed, as ten and La Mejicana tore down the final stretch, pushing and pushing, snorting and snorting, and La Mejicana seemed to accelerate in the final yards, but ten, blasted ten, leapt more than galloped, furiously, and won by a hair.

He felt a sequence of sorrows before anger. The sorrow of this defeat, which for a moment was the only defeat in the world, the sorrow of the lonesomeness known only to those who lose, and the sorrow of false hope. Then came anger.

"Tell me you didn't bet it all."

Pepe gazed at the horse like it was a boat that had set sail the second before his arrival.

"No, not all of it," he said. "Well, not all of yours, just mine; mine, yes, all of it."

"A trumpet in a tavern—*in a tavern*—who ever heard of such a thing?" asked Arriaga. "Trumpets are meant for concert halls."

"Or soldiers," added Mata.

They'd finally decided to go to a coffeeshop. Or in theory that's what it was, a shop for coffee, but everyone there was either already drunk or well on their way. At the back of the establishment, the band: clarinet, violin, some sort of guitar—short on one end, long on the other—and a trumpet. Brass Band said a sign behind them. The band played almost without pause, you could hardly tell the end of one song from the beginning of another, and they were mixing popular dance tunes with snatches of famous operas.

"That's Verdi, that's Mozart, that's Rossini," roiled Arriaga.

"I heard about this," said Ocampo. "It's in fashion."

"What's in fashion is not synonymous with what's good," said Mata.

"And what people call good is sometimes synonymous with what's dying," replied Ocampo.

The last thing he recalls with any clarity is the night he was coming back from the printshop and passed a theater with two distinct streams of people entering and exiting: those exiting, formal, men in sensible hats, women who removed shoes before setting foot on the sidewalk so as not to soil them; those entering, more colorful, both faces and attire, and a sort of strut.

He knows why he didn't say, even for a second, no sir, not me, not at my age, and instead simply shrank, literally shrank, made himself as small as he had been when he first went to Oaxaca, with no manners and no Spanish, and snuck in where he wasn't wanted, to have a little look-see, or a little something to eat, without being seen. If there was one thing he'd learned, and then spent the rest of his life reconfirming, it was that making yourself invisible wasn't enough, that in addition to ensuring you're unseen, you have to convince the lords and ladies you are unseeing, so they don't feel touched by so much as the brush of your eyelash. He slipped in among those who'd paid to enter the theater, not the theater-theater, where an opera must have ended early to make way for this: an enormous salon where there were probably ten, twenty, thirty, no, more, thirty-some couples dancing quadrilles and then polkas and then mazurkas. All around the hall were tables at which almost no one sat; instead, people stood flirting, drinks in hand. There were other halls too, offshoots of the big ballroom, with more tables, where people did sit, to gamble and keep flirting. And absolutely everyone was drunk.

He got out of there quick despite longing to stay, as had so often happened in places not intended for him. The excess, this terrible excess, the glittering excess; impossible to stay, impossible to leave. What devotion to excess could possibly surpass this?

A block away was another theater. This time he didn't even feel the fear of transgression, just shrank himself and blended in with the crowd, and this one actually was a concert hall, no dancing soirees here. But on the first floor there was no way to blend in with the wall; a sentry stopped him on his way in, pointing to the stairs; he walked up to the gallery.

The stage was filled with a single instrument, ten of them, all the same. Pianos. Ten pianos. Nine in a semicircle, each with its respective pianist seated on a stool, and the last in the center, unoccupied. What on earth. A man in frockcoat came out onstage and bowed before the audience, who applauded feverishly, though he'd yet to do a thing.

"Gottschalk," someone beside him said in reverence.

He knew the man's name but not his deeds.

Gottschalk took a seat at the first piano and began to play timidly, like someone peeping through a door, and then he crosshanded some dainty notes, like someone hopping lightly through the door, then immediately gained confidence, like one gaining confidence, and began running his hands up and down the entire keyboard, as if anxious that someone might steal a key, and then he made a sudden sign and a second piano began to telegraph a dreamier melody until it took note of the first one and joined in, and one by one the other pianos also began to join in, chaotically, until finally they synced up in one patriotic song, and the entire audience stood singing, hands to hearts, and then, abruptly, nine pianos fell silent and Gottschalk started to play the overture to *Don Giovanni*, and was interrupted by the second piano playing the overture to *Norma*, and the audience laughed and the musicians all started playing at once, the way they had at the coffeeshop, but this time it was pianos, ten pianos, playing different overtures. It was just like at the coffeeshop, one continuous, absurd song: Gottschalk would silence some pianos and authorize others, one by one, all ten of them, without stopping. The audience clapped and shouted whenever they wanted, becoming part of the concert.

He'd never seen anything like it. Who had ever seen anything like it.

Was it that same night, after he returned, so moved by the music?
    Or was it the next
    or were there several nexts
    or was it a week later
that Ocampo sidled up to him, smiling, with an innocuous, dainty, elegant glass, filled to the brim, and said:
    Try it
    he said
    it's not liquor
    he said
    it's absinthe

he said:

You'll survive.

It was a bear fight. He was at a bear fight. Two black bears, shackled, ringed at the neck by the white man at the end of a chain. They roared and swiped at each other with their paws, thrusting their bear bodies forward. Whenever they stopped, the man would menace them with a stick. A crowd surrounded the bears, jeering. Another man took bets.

He pushed his way out of the circle and searched for one of his compadres. None were in sight. When had he last seen them?

At a coffeeshop, they'd been together. When? Not that day. When? They'd had coffee. Then Mata had bought a round of whiskies and he'd declined, Arriaga bought the second round and he'd declined, Ocampo bought the third and he'd declined, the fourth round was his turn so in all likelihood he'd have drunk that one to be polite . . . or was it from the first round that he'd drunk?, there was no fifth round, not so much because Pepe lacked the cash to cover it but because

there was an enormous fire, and they raced out, followed its glow several blocks to a building ablaze, and Arriaga, standing a few yards away, said My God, I know what this is, it's an orphanage for girls; no sooner had the words left his mouth than the girls ran out, terrified, and a crowd of people turned up, pulling out buckets from who knows where and passing them down a spontaneously formed line in an attempt to put out the flames, until the fire wagons arrived, horses pulling so furiously it was as if their snorting might extinguish the flames;

all of this they saw, he and his compadres: yes, the others were still there for that, but were no longer there for the dead body, because

there was a dead body, when?, it was just him and Pepe one morning, a morning damp with fog, when they came upon a small and hungover crowd gathered beside a gangway; a man had fallen in between two boats, but by the time he realized it and started splashing around, the boats had gutted him, and there was a guy trying to recover his guts as though they were still a man; the others hadn't seen that, no, he'd seen the others somewhere else, because

there was still another spot, not a coffeeshop, somewhere darker and more claustrophobic that smelled not like coffee but like—what?, what was that smell? . . . Holy mother, it was a brothel, a brothel, he'd never been to one before but the way couples were loveydoving right out in the open, no way could folks carry on like that anywhere but a brothel; those damn cads, vipers, they were snakes in the grass, even though *he* was the one who'd always been called a snake, an Indian snake, as if being in politics meant betraying his people, but look: whose slithery idea had it been to come here? At some point he thought he saw Ocampo but then lost him; at another, he thought he saw Arriaga and that Arriaga had seen him, but . . . had the man hidden? Had Arriaga slipped off? How long had he been there? Was that the day he went to the printshop and then, so dazzled by the old quadrant, forgot to come back?

there was wandering about, dizzle-dazzled by the shop with the daguerreotypes, which you could see through the windows, and the firefighters' parade, where they played instruments and the public applauded them like heroes, and the hot-air balloons flying over the city. Before setting out on this delivery, which took who knows how long, which was apparently ongoing, he saw the date on the printshop paper and said to himself Tomorrow's the start of Lent, Ash Wednesday, and what didn't occur to him was that this meant today was Fat Tuesday, today was Mardi Gras; he read the news of a bigamist called to account, of several women sent to the loony bin for, the paper said, being unable to take charge of themselves, of a man who turned his son in to the police for being a bad and ungovernable boy, to be put into a place called the Home Shelter till he turned twenty-one. Odd: with so many crazies and so many ungovernables, certain women and certain men had no right to be so; there was something important in that, something he was beginning to see; and then later—or perhaps it was earlier?

there were parades, spontaneous parades that poured into the streets and sometimes merged and headed off in the same direction and sometimes squeezed to one side of the street and pressed on in their initial direction; and a procession of people: he's walking outside the old quadrant once again and he's not alone, who's he with?, he's with other people, not looking at them, but instead looking down at his muddy feet; and then the city lights, which had disappeared from sight, reappeared, more makeshift now, atop rough-and-ready shacks and stalls selling food and booze to anyone with scratch, including the captured, and there were bonfires and drums. Drums. The ones he'd heard earlier. He'd found them. Long drums, tall drums, itty-bitty drums, all making a tremendous racket, a group of women at the center waving kerchiefs, but so many other folks too, black and whitewashed and even a few white but mostly black, also dancing, not quadrilles, not polkas, not mazurkas, but something in a language he didn't know, a new grammar of bones, no one dancing as a couple and no one dancing alone, and yet they were not an undifferentiated mass but a large number of people composing a single strophe, a verse, a *stanza* as the Italians say: a room. Beside him, a man more fancified than befit that particular room looked upon it all in anger, then looked at him as if to say, What do you expect?, and then, clear as day, as if by saying so he were climbing atop a box and looking down on the others, said:

"The canaille."

And left. The canaille. There they were. The room was not a place. It was them. It was him.

And there was some meandering through the swamp, where he heard nothing but the splash of his own footsteps and sounds for which he had no name—birds, reptiles, plants, water?—nothing was still, until he came to a more solid part and kept walking and happened upon the bear fight.

None of his companions were there. He got out as fast as he could, feeling that these were experiences he had no right to, the roaring distress of the bears, but also the portent of the drums, but also the swampiness of those chaotic days as well as the swamp-swamp beneath his feet, but also that trumpet like a spike of wind at the coffeeshop, but the brothel, but the pianos, but the sound, the unbearable sound hammering his brain so loud that when he finally reached the old quadrant he didn't even recognize it, it had all become the clamor of celebration, it was all foreign, he turned down a street, did not know it, turned down two others, did not know them, walked on for several blocks, slipped down an alley, which he suddenly realized was not an alley but the walkway to a house, which led to the silence, and the stillness, of an inner courtyard.

There were no chairs in this courtyard. Well, there was one, but tucked ever so daintily into a corner, veritably hidden among vines that climbed up three floors, caressing the walls more than distressing them, planters in bloom like it wasn't December, all of it alive and yet quiet and subtle, like some sort of swamp utopia.

He heard footsteps from within the house and retreated to the walkway; two men came down a staircase that led straight to the street, and did not see him.

He left without closing the gate.

Several people, men and women, were seated at the long table, not like folks who'd come for breakfast but like folks who'd stayed for breakfast, still drinking. Thisbee told him to sit and when she got close to him she scrunched up her nose and smiled:

"Funk," she said.

Eh? What?

"Funk. That smell," she said, and he understood because she made signs for each word: "the smell of sweat, the smell of tobacco," and he also understood the next thing even without any signs:

"The masters can't stand it."

The next morning two policemen came and took Thisbee away in cuffs, accused of harboring a woman who was not her property.

THREE

Sure, they were outlaws; after all, that's the reason they were there. But to be *called* outlaws, well, that was another matter. A person has the right to defend their honor with one hand while hiding a dagger in the other. They were outlaws not just because they were pariahs and undesirables but because of things their enemies didn't even suspect: going to brothels, perverting the course of justice, being the canaille; and, who'd have thought, also because they themselves would end up asking to be surveilled like the conspirators they were. What they didn't know, though, the worst thing of all, which they discovered after all the rest, was that theirs was a conspiracy of extras.

Under the roofs of the edifice of Law is a guard who will let in anyone wanting to enter, not because they might benefit from the Law but because under this roof the canaille are no longer a concern and become simply a heap of humans with ragged lives; outside, things were different, but here inside they're all just bums, as is he, walking among forgers, prostitutes, drunks, thieves, some cuffed, others packed in any which way; even the police, differentiated only by their badges, in all other ways were kitted out like the canaille.

Ocampo snuck into a chamber to try and understand how this Law worked, while *he* studied the people it oppressed.

"This is no court of law," Ocampo said, "it's something else. There are no judges here; just people who determine the preliminary fate of the accused before sending them on to a judge."

Ocampo led him by the arm to the door of one of the chambers and pointed to a man at the back.

"The head honchos are these men called Recorders, or Registrars, who decide which court each person is sent to, or rather, the ones who are considered persons; slaves and free people of color are judged and sentenced right here. Doesn't look good."

But then Ocampo held up a finger in roguish enthusiasm.

"But there are two things stacked in our favor. One, I saw that if for any reason the attorney assigned to a case doesn't show up, the charge is dismissed. And two, your landlady was arrested in the third ward."

"So?"

"So the third ward is the most corrupt."

"But we can't offer money to a civil servant," he said.

"We're not going to offer him money. I mean, we're going to offer him something, but we won't give him anything. We figure out who the prosecutor on duty is, feel him out, and then find a way to distract him. This will require a good story."

So we're going to break the law, he thought, but then refuted his own assertion with sham scientificity: well, actually we're just going to bend it slightly.

He set off to find the prop they needed, with no idea how to pay for it (though he managed); meanwhile, with a coin, Ocampo convinced a guard to let him know when the prosecutor arrived. Then they waited for the man at his chambers, and as soon as he appeared, at the end of the long corridor, they knew their plan had a chance: the prosecutor was plodding down the hall with a hangover plain as a crown of cactus, and, more important, his clothes made clear that he had nobody at home to say You look like a pile of dirty sheets.

"An-*toine*," Ocampo exclaimed, approaching, arms wide, and then in overly affected French, "just in time; let's go."

Antoine looked confused but held on to what little dignity he still had, focused on Ocampo, and stammered Quoi? Ocampo guffawed.

"Yesterday you couldn't stop speaking French," Ocampo said in English. "And might I say, your accent is magnificent."

Antoine waved off the compliment with one hand but also grinned, conceding the possibility.

"At any rate," Ocampo continued, "it's time."

The prosecutor stared at Ocampo, clearly attempting to recall the matter Ocampo was so assuredly referring to without letting on that he had no clue.

Ocampo leaned in and whispered:

"Le plaçage."

This part had been *his* idea. He recalled Cabañas telling him about the local custom by which free mothers and creoles would sometimes offer one of their daughters to a powerful white man. As a concubine, not a wife, since she's not totally white, Cabañas had clarified, but white enough to be a regular companion, which means she has to be a quadroon or octo-roon; who knows how the accuracy of these fractions can be verified, there's no way to confirm it, all anyone can do is trust what they're told in confidence; anyway, what matters is that her color is noticeable, because that's the charm of a placée—that's what they're called—though not too noticeable. A man might spend half the week with his official wife and the other half with the extra. They work it all out in advance, negotiating the terms of the contract: what to do about the children, what the placée will receive. It's quite complicated, Cabañas had added after a pause.

The daguerreotype had been his idea too. Ocampo now showed it to the prosecutor.

"Voilà: just what you requested last night."

Antoine gazed at the woman in the daguerreotype, fascinated and fearful in equal measure.

"Her mother awaits us. As you might imagine, the girl has a number of suitors, but I've convinced her mother that you're the ideal candidate."

The prosecutor eyed his chambers.

"Ah, don't you worry, nothing pressing here, only trivial matters; I already checked."

Ocampo led Antoine gently by the arm, like someone offering a tour of a palace, then spent the entire walk singing the praises of plaçage.

They took him to a tavern on the far side of the old quadrant. By the time they arrived it was likely that enough time had passed for Thisbee's case to be dismissed, but they bought him five shots just the same, all at once, and set each one on the table. Then Ocampo said:

46

"Let me go see if the young lady is ready, the place is just over the road. I might take a minute, but don't worry, you know what women are like."

The prosecutor smiled in doleful delusion, and with a trembling hand lifted the first shot to his lips.

"He'll find love someday," Ocampo said when they walked out, "or something like it. If there's one good reason not to show up at work, that's it."

Some of the coffeeshops had copies of living papers, but they were all in English, and though he was understanding more and more, he missed the meat and marrow of living papers in Spanish. So he'd head to the levee to see how or from whom he might obtain papers from home; sometimes he had to pay, other times they were given to him for free, especially when he didn't ask if he could have them for free; just sheer patience, sheer forbearance, until it became clear no one was going to buy them, and then the stevedores would give him a look and, in curiosity and sometimes even respect, hand him the papers.

(And on the occasions when he did ask, he did so without begging; he never begged, not even when writing I beg you in an official document, which unlike a living paper is a tombstone, an impossibly thin grave etched in haughty grammar and a language spoken by no one. Dead papers exist only to necrofy life, to create the illusion that it can be contained and archived. Dead papers abound in endpoints, in full stops. Living papers, on the other hand, arrive all nice and warm, bleeding ink, showcasing stories, insinuating endings, endearing themselves to all, cliffhanging the troubles of the day before, foretelling those of the day to come.)

47

Local living papers were things he read in order to corroborate what he'd seen, because the written word convinces you of the impossible, from moving worlds, transcribed as climate, to the movement of people, reported as drama.

Living papers that came from Mexico seemed anxious to stretch their bones and say what they'd come to say, which, in this particular case—what a fucking farce—was that the dictator had sent a delegation to Cuba for the express purpose of drumming up soldiers for an Imperial Guard. He laughed wholeheartedly: pathetic one-legged dipshit. Then laughed brokenheartedly: how he longed to be there now, not recruiting soldiers or thinking about empire but about words less majestic, sipping his coffee and eating his sweet bun, bent over news that was not so dispiriting.

The newspaper had also reported, while they were lost out there in the swamp, that Juan Álvarez, Ignacio Comonfort, and Florencio Villarreal had proclaimed the Plan of Ayutla, from Guerrero. Time for ole one-leg to go, it said, albeit with fancier words, time for him to go and take his bootlickers with him.

Doctor Borrego held up a pair of pliers that resembled enormous ice tongs and said:

"Don't move, this is going to take a minute."

The doctor was moving the instrument all around his skull, measuring, taking notes.

Cabañas had taken him and Pepe to see Doctor Borrego.

"Business drops off after Carnival season, so for several months I won't be able to pay an assistant," he told them, "but

I'll introduce you to someone who's always in need of cheap labor."

Which he did, though they still hadn't discussed any type of employment. As soon as Borrego saw him, he'd said Take a seat, and began his cranial examination. His was a sorry-looking practice, with one table, a cot, and a few vaguely medical implements hanging on the wall. A curtain screened off the practice from another area.

"What is all this?" he finally asked.

"Phrenology," Borrego replied, spitting the word more than saying it. "All the rage. Allows one to determine a person's vices and passions by measuring the shape of their skull."

"And does it work?"

Borrego gaped, incredulous.

"Of course not. Eight out of ten things I sell don't work in the slightest, but I need to be familiar with them all the same."

"What are the other two, the ones that do?"

"Well, there's this one," he said sticking out his tongue. "Persuasion. Anybody who can be persuaded that they can be cured, can be cured, at least for a while."

A while. Un ratito. Instead of a while he'd said un ratito. Borrego spoke Spanish, but in an accent like none he'd ever heard; the man might have been from the antipodes, or from some bygone era, or from an era that had never existed at all.

"And the tenth?"

Borrego took two steps over to the curtain and drew it back with a flourish.

"This."

It was another room, with two tables; on one lay a few

broad, crescent-shaped knives, some cylinders, and tobacco, so much tobacco.

"This is the real deal. Cigars. Puros. Genuine Cuban. Though made here, behind the curtain; you know, licenses and all that foolishness. Interested?"

One minute Jackson Square was a town square, and the next it was a deserted square: first joyous, noisy, bustling, smelly, and then all flat and drab. He and Ocampo were smoking, Arriaga was kneading his fists as he spoke; they'd been immersed in conspiracy for most of the afternoon when they heard cannon fire. They'd turned their heads toward the boom but couldn't see where the sound had come from. And when they turned, a precise yet mysterious activity was underway: it wasn't that everyone was in motion, it was that some remained still while others began determinedly walking away from the center of the square. Not the idlers: the carters; not the frockcoats: the loose shirts; not the white and whitened but the black and blackened. It took him a minute to pick up on the pattern, which became undeniably clear when a badge approached, slow and circumspect and chewing chaw. The officer came to a stop in front of them, looked from one to the next, still sitting on their bench, and then, eyes flitting back and forth between Arriaga and Ocampo, said:

"Who's this one belong to?"

This one understood the intention of the tongue, understood the pointed finger. And Arriaga explained what the officer said next.

"You do know he can be here after eight only in the company of his owner or with written permission."

None of them replied.

"Or did you not hear the cannon?"

Then the officer did a double take, stepping out of the light so as to observe him with greater attention. The cop put his hands on his waist and leaned toward him as though studying a bug. Then said:

"Wha . . . ? You ain't . . . Wait, all dressed like that . . . What are you?" He turned to the others. "What is he?"

"Mexican," said Arriaga, in English.

The officer raised his eyebrows as if to say what in tarnation. "Ha!" he said.

And then turned and carried on patrolling the plaza.

Houses optimistically elevated on stone or broke-brick pilings, three hands of air between floor and earth so the water would excuse them whenever the river overflowed. After returning from their undertakings, the two of them would sit on the steps of the boat-house. Thisbee would give him free coffee, and he'd slip her cigars when he could. By way of mmms and ahhhms they commented on the coffee and the tobacco, greeted folks passing by, and pointed out things of note: a dog, a cup, the smoke, each saying the word for it in their tongue.

Later came the less point-outable: stories about something that had happened that day, or long ago. On one of those occasions, he pointed to the room he'd seen Thisbee in with the girl. Who is she? Thisbee shot him an obligatory look of suspicion and yet right away decided to tell him, with gestures, and some words they shared, and others to be intuited.

"She's not from here, the poor woman was stolen from a

place she was free, to be sold here. One day I found her and she came with me."

Thisbee said nothing about where it was she'd seen her or what all she'd had to do to free her, as if it were—as in fact it was—simply a matter of making up one's mind.

"Have you helped others?"

Thisbee looked inward, like a piano trilling on the low notes, and exhaled a puff of smoke.

There's something about machines that cancels out superstition. A machine doesn't speculate. A machine holds no bias. A machine has no convictions or desires. A machine operates on facts. The facts of cause and consequence. The fact of volume, the fact of density. The fact of metal. Machines are the form of the world's intelligence.

On this much they agreed.

"That's the very principle we should use to govern society," said Ocampo. "The laws of physics are the laws of the people."

"People aren't made of steel," he said. "People need meaning, they need direction."

"Machines have direction."

"Machines have inevitability: they can't make decisions. They do what they do inexorably."

"Not only that," said Arriaga. "People have got to have something of **their own**, something besides explanations—scientific or spiritual, makes no difference. What does make a difference is having a place that belongs to them from which to determine their direction. **Their land.**"

"The people should have the land, that's fair and just," he said, "but they also need to know what they want it for."

"That could take a lifetime, it's already taken many lifetimes," said Ocampo, "which is why those who are underdogs don't know what to do with it. The real problem is **too few producers and too many idlers**. Property in the hands of the Church is idle property."

"The same goes for **large landowners**," Arriaga added.

"The same goes for **large landowners**," Ocampo agreed. "**Saint Simon** says something along those lines. Have you read him? **Saint Simon**. Says that if every unproductive person in a country were suddenly to disappear, the country would lose nothing."

"What about **people who lack the means of production?**" asked Arriaga.

"Ah, well, that's why we need to abolish inheritance, among other things. Inheritance does nothing but perpetuate the number of people who are unproductive," said Ocampo.

He agreed, but Arriaga squinted skeptically and said:

"Not all inheritance is equal. Not all of it is only the patrimony of the head of family."

"That's what I'm saying: we must study society the same way we study the rest of nature. Understanding *this*"—he took in the entire square with his gesture—"is going to prove useful, even if it feels like we're in limbo right now." Arriaga turned to him. "You work at a printer's, right?"

"Used to. We're rolling cigars now, me and Pepe."

"I'm training to be a pot maker."

He and Arriaga stared at Ocampo in shock.

"But you have savings."

"Some. But what good is having them without knowing what they're *for*?" He smiled. "In order to understand society, one needs to experience the realities of different social classes."

"I don't think a class is something one simply goes to visit," he said.

"Perhaps not. But one can learn more by hammering metal than by praying to a crucifix."

And that was when they heard the cannon.

He and Thisbee also spoke of things that can only be pointed to at the risk of shriveling a finger, things better left in peace if they can't be changed, even though they're never really at peace and are in fact like hordes pressing at a door. More than words, what these things called for was a delicate touch, and time.

There was, or there had been, a small child who was no longer, or who was no longer there. Thisbee mentioned him in a tone that invited no further inquiry.

He had a family and he'd had a family. One was lonely and alone, shaken and devastated. The other, the one he'd left behind, he almost never mentioned.

To shake off their sorrow, she explained how they obtained the planks to build houses from ships run aground. He told her about living with his uncle Bernardino in the mountains, and about the time he spent an entire night floating in a lagoon called the Enchanted Lagoon, and that he used to be afraid of dying, but that night he'd seen the lucidity of the elements, seen that the whole world was made up only of elements, and it was best to face them.

Later that night, hovering on the edge of sleep, he realized that he'd said yelha for lagoon when speaking with her, *yelha,* in **Didza**, which was the way he said it to himself, never aloud.

His first days at the cigar workshop had been a total retreat inward, the contemplation of a drop of water that contains all the images of the world but doesn't allow them to be seen or thought: just a drop of liquid, plip-plipping away the hours. The days after that had been a foray into his hands, into what they were learning to do, into how they hurt, into their color and the color of the tobacco, into the smell of the tobacco, which became the smell of his hands, into the whole arduous hustle that was coming to fruition; the routine of stretching, rolling, cutting, wrapping, hours spent thinking with his hands about what to do next: not merely to support Álvarez and try not to dominate him; the others failed to see that though Álvarez was not booksish, he was brainy, the man was way too cool to fool, and, yes, they had to support Vidaurri, but more than that they had to keep an eye on his sticky fingers; and they needed a plan in place for when the dictator fell, because fall he would, as sure as night falls, but so what, so what, there'd already been too damn many clever little men who'd pushed out the one in place and then not known what needed to be done. Here's what needs to be done, he thought with his hands: hustle, put out one reform, then another, shake things up before the conservatives realize they're already shook. In his head, which was his hands, again and again he ran through the stages, the battles, the words, the dates that were needed to set in motion all that was to come, and even if things didn't turn out that way, then, in an orderly process, it would still be an arrow fired, an arrow made with the mind in his hands.

Then came a different sort of day, another retreat inward, but this time a different inward, one more concrete and terrifying than any battle or conspiracy, a diving down more than a retreat, into himself and his debts, debts of valor and of love, falling through his own cracks, the crack of his pride, the crack of his loneliness, the crack of his emptiness. His two families, no longer a first and a second in either time or importance, now both second to his wretched troubles, troubles that had gotten him locked up and thrown onto one ship and then another ship and then landed him in this swamp and this room full of leaves.

Which was why he asked Borrego to scupper the silence.

"Doctor, I have an idea, tell me what you think."

Borrego, who'd been courting a snooze in his armchair, stirred slightly, just an eye and one finger, which he raised from his belly, where it lay in a sign of Go on.

"When I was in Cuba, I visited a cigar factory, you know that, but there's something I didn't tell you."

Borrego opened the other eye.

"While the workers are rolling leaves, someone else helps them by reading aloud, so they don't get bored."

"Reading? Reading what?"

"Poems. Fables. Historical tales."

Borrego raised his head a bit, then tilted it toward him one more bit.

"You want me to read you poems?"

"It doesn't have to be poems, it could be something else."

"No, no, I'm not really a book person, per se, plus there's my eye strain."

Borrego nodded off again but suddenly opened both eyes and said, with something approaching enthusiasm:

"I could tell my own stories, though, now, that I could do."

Hearing this, Pepe lifted his head too.

"I can tell you things I'd never tell anybody . . . And you two," he added, looking at them in kindly contempt, "hiding out here, hardly speaking any English, you're like nobodies."

Suddenly spry, he shot up from his wicker chair, dragged it over, sat back down, and said:

"Now then."

Sometimes when they had a little cash to spare, they'd try coffeeshops outside the old quadrant, ones that were more affordable and less fancy, ones that also had music but just one or two players, rarely a whole band, places they could go to talk or just prick up their ears; and in the underbrush of tongues, every so often they detected someone speaking Spanish.

They sat in a corner, as usual, and lit their cigars. The late crowd had yet to arrive, and it was still more café than cantina, meaning it was possible to walk between tables, even make out what people were saying. That was how he heard a voice speaking Spanish; he couldn't piece together everything it said, but he noted the vivid diction of his own tongue, though with a certain singsong gulfiness to it. It was coming from the far side of the coffeeshop. He turned to Pepe to see whether he wanted to join him, but Pepe was fumbling along in bettered French with a meagerly clad, brown-skinned señorita who didn't know whether to stay or go, so he did them a favor and stood.

He followed the trail of words, the sturdy vowels and dropped esses, through a splinter of speech: "Protestantism, as you know, is not at the vanguard of enlightenment, no religion is, but when compared to Catholicism it's a breath of fresh air; set beside the Christianity of ignorance, it is the Christianity of civilization."

This was when he discovered that coffeeshops were also a good way to get educated.

It was a kid speaking. Beard. Coat and vest. Sophisticated vocabulary. A bearded, serious, elegant young man, but a kid all the same, standing before five or six others, who sat there listening, and two or three more, who seemed only to be pretending to listen but didn't leave. Maybe not everyone understood what the kid was talking about, but there was something in his emphasis, in his aim, in the way he addressed each word to his audience's chests, literally, hand straight out, chopping the air with it; no one left.

He was talking about Cuba. And it was clear this wasn't the first time he'd preached on Cuba. The history of Cuba before Cuba, its original inhabitants slaughtered by the cross, the endless tedium of the colony. And then the kid surprised him by making an observation that he himself had read someplace but never heard expressed quite so plainly:

"And know this, my *American* friends—and I'm referring to Americans from *this* country—Spain's defeat will not be your gain, no. Because it's already being talked about, right? 'We have to oust those decadent Spaniards,' isn't that so? Sure, yes, kick them out, give them the boot, but don't do it so that you can take their place, don't do it so you can take Cuba and turn it into a slave colony, as your congressmen are already discussing. No, sirs, seek not that profit from us."

When the kid had finished, he swept his eyes across the crowd as if waiting to see whether anyone might want to refute him, but the few who were actually listening seemed either to be in agreement or attempting to understand. The kid fixed his gaze on *him* for a moment, in fleeting curiosity, and then unfixed it and started shuffling the papers on which his ideas were registered.

He sipped his coffee and decided to finish his cigar back at the table, where he found Pepe's coffee, still steaming, but neither hide nor hair of Pepe himself. The man's location was anyone's guess; he'd often disappear, who knows where, and say he'd only been out for a stroll.

"This reminds me of a story about my friend Serge," Borrego said, "back when he was an attorney. Not that he ever stopped being one or in fact ever was one to begin with: back then Serge was whatever he needed to be. The man talked like an attorney, dressed like an attorney, impressed like an attorney. He'd slip into courthouses to hunt down property disputes. Convince each party to leave matters in his hands and leave the property altogether while he took care of things; then he'd move in for months, till the various owners got fed up, and move out like nothing had happened."

Borrego recalled this after the two of them had gone to the edifice of Law; the doctor had asked him to come along in order to advise an attorney friend—a real one—on a matter involving land. It was a conflict in California being litigated here, who knows why, and the documents were in Spanish. Turned out to be a simple affair, a property-line dispute he'd cleared up in no time, which mightily impressed the court officials, who had looked on in wonder as expertise issued forth from a man—him—so slight and small and blended-in with the wall. It made Borrego come off well, so Borrego had given him an extra cigar and then remembered his friend Serge.

"Smart guy, Serge, always has interesting business at hand."

"So he's your associate."

"I have many friends and even more associates. The sagacious life that some of us lead can't be led without associates. Don't believe all that nonsense about a few bad apples spoiling the good. Good apples are only good for show; the product you sell, those're the bad ones. And to display a pretty truth while selling a filthy one takes teamwork."

"So how did you meet this associate?"

"Oh, professionally. He turned up one day with his hands burned after setting fire to his house—for the insurance, heh-heh. I treated him, he paid me handsomely, and we became friends. Strange are the ways of providence," Borrego concluded, whatever the man meant by *providence*.

The copy of *El Universal* he'd picked up at the levee contained a poisonous story about them, though as usual it didn't mention him by name. The article called them vile instruments of petty vengeance, accused them of recruiting pirates to invade the country; of wanting to abolish religion, morality, and tradition; of professing the religion of Voltaire and the doctrines of Danton and Marat.

Small swell of pride at allegedly being so cogent, but the

consequences of reports like that were noxious. He was outraged and went to tell the others what an outrage it was, and
together they raged out: such an indignity, what an affront,
such lies, what to do. Letters. Write letters! They wrote letters
of rebuttal to send to Mexico, and a letter to the Mexican consul in the city demanding that the consul deny the allegations
since he knew them to be untrue, since he already had them
under surveillance—which might or might not have been the
case, but safer to assume that it was—as well as letters to the
mayor and the chief of police asking them to certify that they
were neither conspiring nor recruiting pirates. Letters all written in arrogant calligraphy, in majestic prose, in outraged astonishment. In none did they include his name, two or three
signatures would suffice, no need to draw attention away from
the substance. Pepe took note of the signatories, and, though
he wasn't in the room, he heard Pepe say:

"They're always belittling Benito, that's why he kicks everyone's ass in the end."

"Those chinaco guerillas are here," said the secretary to the
consul, opening the door just a crack so the visitors couldn't
peek in. The consul must have said Send them in, because he
sent them in: Mata, Ocampo, and himself.

Arrangoiz, the consul, had a broad forehead and curly side-
burns that dripped down to his jowls. Years earlier he'd disappeared some funds, secured from a bank, that had been
intended for Mexico. Arrangoiz stood before them and neither sat nor offered them a seat. They glared at one another in
ceremonious hatred for a few seconds.

"Our business here is so brief," Ocampo began, as if he in

fact had no desire to sit, "that we've come merely to hand you a duplicate of the letter we previously sent and to which we have received no reply."

Arrangoiz let out a couple of snorts before replying.

"I don't work for you lot." The consul said *you lot* as if the words sullied his tongue and had to be spat out. "And I won't deign to provide a written reply, so you will have to settle for this: regardless of what I may know about what you've planned or plotted, or what I know about what you're now planning or plotting against the government of Mexico, it is to the government and not *you lot* that I must render account. And your letter has been remitted to the government."

"You can send this one as well; that will suffice," Ocampo said.

They stood in silence, unsure of the etiquette for taking leave of someone you despise. Then they turned and walked out.

W. H. James, the chief of police, had sent J. N. Lewis, mayor of the city, a document stating that he'd investigated the matter and attesting to the fact that he'd found no evidence that the accusations against the Exiles bore any truth. The mayor added a note, which he signed, saying the report was credible and authoritative.

Mata read both documents aloud and they cheered raucously, shouting Yessir! and Damn right! Then they congratulated each other in more measured tones, and then they fell silent. Because although they didn't say so, it had suddenly dawned on them that the worst part was that it was *true*: they weren't doing anything.

As if that weren't enough, as they'd fittingly presumed, from then on they were also under surveillance.

"I expect you saw what happened on election day," said Borrego, "the thugs at the polls, the fights, the casualties. Did you see that a police officer got stabbed? That's why Serge and I quit. Not for lack of work, but lack of commitment. And prudence. Two or three times we managed to nab slaves on the lam to resell, but once, we ran into the owner of the slave we were selling. We could've insisted he was ours, but we had no papers and the owner had a pistol, so we politely withdrew. Counterfeiting is something else to avoid getting mixed up in, too risky, but if, say, you fabricate tickets for steamships and sell them yourself, well, that's both a quick profit and a service to the community. If you two ever need to travel, just say the word."

"Was there a reason we all had to come?" asked Mata, attempting unsuccessfully to cross one leg over the other. He glanced at the others as if repeating the question or waiting for someone to move: Mata himself, Ocampo, Arriaga, or him. Pepe had stayed behind, but the others didn't see this as an absence; they saw him as a small dog, or a child. They were finally attempting to become what they'd been accused of being.

All four were crowded onto the only wooden raft they could afford; the raftsman stood rowing at the front, with them behind, pressed together like some multilegged beast.

"These things can't be decided by one person alone; this is no small matter," said Ocampo.

As soon as they left the river and entered the bayou, the landscape grew denser, twitchier, closer, as if the trees had bent over to give them a sniff. For a while there was no sign of people aside from a hut hidden in the swampland and a couple of placards that were no longer legible. Vipers coiled around trees, a few gators lolled at the water's edge, others slid along parallel to the raft. When they worried the gators were getting too close, the men would press together even tighter and the raftsman would laugh.

To distract himself, he asked:

"What's the name of the place we're going?"

"Barataria," Arriaga said.

He turned, incredulous, to stare at Arriaga.

"Yep." Arriaga smiled.

"But how can that be? They named part of the swamp after the island Sancho Panza governs in *Don Quijote*?"

"Seems so."

"Who, though? The pirates? I mean, pirates were the ones who established this place, right?"

"Jean Lafitte," said Ocampo. "This was his center of operations, though he had an office in the city center. I'm serious: that's where he'd receive people. He helped this bunch"—*this* meaning the Americans—"fight the British, and after that they never messed with him again."

A branch appeared at throatslitting speed and everyone instinctively ducked.

"So Jean Lafitte read *Don Quijote*?"

"It wasn't named after *Don Quijote*," said Arriaga. "The name comes from selling stuff cheap, barato. Originally it was Barateur, which somehow evolved into Barataria. A lot of people who live here came from the Canaries, so that may be it."

They remained silent for several seconds in the wake of Arriaga's insight.

"Or . . . maybe, maybe," he said, absurdly amused, "some pirate read *Don Quijote.*"

Barataria was a less sturdy, more rough-and-ready, less traveled, more makeshift, less policed version of the city's port, which was itself chaotic and rough-and-ready, although not makeshift. Two ships sat in the bay, but the action was all on shore, selling linen, spices, wood, wine, rum, medicine. People.

"That pirate might be dead, but it sure seems like he's still hanging around," said Ocampo. "Do pirates exist anymore?"

"There will always be pirates," said Arriaga, "they're simply better dressed these days. The ones around here are just starting to save up for suits. But before long they'll turn up in the city with aristocratic titles."

Vendors approached, offered their products—almost always to Ocampo. They'd all worn their best suits, which by now were plenty worse for wear, but only Ocampo's still had a whiff of well-to-do.

"Let's go," Mata prodded, urging them on with his eyes. He'd been out here before, to find out who they might do business with. Mata also had a few bodies under his belt, from back in 1847, during the US invasion, when both his medical knowledge and his marksmanship had been put to good use.

But *he* was still not persuaded. Not that what they were doing was unnecessary, but it was vital that they agree on the decisions to be made after their victory. And yet it was as if the others had astigmatism: since everything was blurry, they decided to shoot at whatever was in front of them. Plus, he wasn't convinced there was no way to negotiate. The tyrant was growing weaker by the day, and soon even his most loyal would start to turn.

"Who do you want at the table when we sit down to talk?" asked Ocampo, and then reminded him of facts that even he could not refute. "Who was the most educated, refined, intelligent man of them all? Lucas Alamán. And what did Alamán do?"

What did Alamán do. He knew what Alamán had done; it still made him sick to think about it. He knew, but Ocampo told him anyway.

"Alamán had Guerrero killed, he had the president killed. The president and those like him. As if they were trash. It wasn't that he hated their ideas, he simply hated being told what to do by plebs. That's who we're dealing with."

And that's why the four of them were there, in the swamp, looking for what they were looking for.

"Come on," said Mata, and they followed him to a stall with a table, the merchandise covered by a cloth. They stood there as if waiting for a watchword. The merchant took their measure with a hint of disappointment and then addressed Mata in French. Mata nodded, and the man pulled back the sheet, revealing several rifles of various calibers.

They began chattering excitedly about the guns, as if they had any idea what they were talking about. Mata was the only one who knew weapons. But they didn't have enough for even the oldest of those on display. All they had was the urge, and the conviction that it was time to get a move on. The whole business with the letters had made it clear that Álvarez had started the revolution, and they had become superfluous politicians, extras.

"Mexicans," someone said behind him.

He turned and saw, a few feet away, the young man who'd spoken at the coffeeshop, looking only at him, not the others.

"Tell them not to buy from the first guy they talk to," he said. "Never a shortage of arms for sale here."

For a second the two of them eyed the others pointing to this or that rifle in childish delight.

"Pedro Santacilia," the kid said, holding out a hand.

"I saw you at the coffeeshop the other day," he replied.

"And I, you. I don't know your story, but my guess is we're in a similar sort of limbo."

He gave a millimetric nod in reply.

Mata was arguing with the merchant, who'd clearly quoted a price that was too high—no matter how low—and Mata looked disappointed.

"We'll talk," he said.

"Yeah, yeah, yeah," the merchant replied in boredom.

Santacilia greeted them all with a nod; they introduced themselves.

"I know people," Santacilia said. "Once you've saved up, I'll introduce you."

And before he left, Santacilia said to him:

"Come by the coffeeshop. We'll think of something."

A drowned man lay on the gurney in Borrego's office. Freshly drowned, not swollen up or fish-nibbled. The man looked more exhausted than dead. His body was there when they arrived, as was someone they later learned was an officer of the court, who was both harried and hurried. Borrego examined the corpse with a show of professionalism, looking into his pupils, tapping his lungs, opening his mouth. Then delivered his verdict:

"Death by drowning."

At least Borrego didn't say it as if he'd solved a great riddle. The court officer walked over to the table, took some things— a watch, a few bills—and left others. Then he went and got another man to help him take the drowned man away.

"We'll have to discuss this another time," Borrego said, once the others had left. "They're doing away with the police department, replacing it with a Police Board. Makes no difference to me, but we'll need to agree upon new terms so they keep bringing poor souls to have their deaths certified, doing that final good deed," he said, slipping his share of the booty into a drawer.

"This isn't a business you split with Serge?"

Borrego simply stared at the wall, as if he could disappear inside it.

"That was Serge."

He and Pepe stared at Borrego in horror.

"Don't look so shocked. It was bound to happen one day. Serge might not have known, but I did. And I knew this was how he was going to die."

"By drowning?"

"By being drowned. Murdered. A witness says he saw a man, at the canal, holding Serge's head underwater, and that the man was the property of Serge. One who'd escaped previously, and that time they caught him for the stupidest thing: imagine, stealing a compass."

He realized they were under surveillance not because they were being surveilled, but because he recognized the one doing the surveilling. The pensive expression, the obvious sloth, the spherical belly. It was the same badge who'd approached them in Jackson Square a few weeks earlier.

He had seen him outside the Hotel Conti, and then at the fruit market too. The guy didn't even hide it: he was a good watcher due to his lack of effort; he'd divert himself, buy something to eat, chitchat. Always in the company of a horse he didn't ride that ambled along behind him like a secretary, or a witness.

They exchanged glances once. The badge's eyes were watery, murky. Something moving slowly beneath the surface.

FOUR

These people farm people, they breed humans captured at birth.

These people fatten up their children, their own children, and then sell them.

These people, crazy with fear as the months tick by and the weather hots up, they run, afraid of another epidemic like the one in 1853, which left piles of half-buried corpses on the ground and orphans wandering the streets. It's coming, time to cut and run, they say, as if they themselves were not the epidemic.

"You need to go," said Thisbee, not in the firm way she said it to customers who didn't shove off after eating, or to the ones who thought that buying a coffee also bought them the right to hang out and encumber; in which case she'd say, with glacial top-doggedness, You need to go.

The *You need to go* she said to them was less an order and more an inevitability. He didn't reply, awaiting some kind of explanation. They were in the kitchen; Thisbee had just hacked a chicken in half and was now extracting its innards.

"I need your room."

She stopped what she was doing, and for one tense minute

it seemed as if she was going to say why. Then everything about her softened—her face, her shoulders, her bloody hands—and she gave them a kind smile.

"And you two need to find another house. You won't survive the summer in this one."

One after the other came a series of señores, all arriving to offer their help, to corrupt him:

first Señor Rivas
then Señor Cebayos
then Señor Ajuria
then Señor Bernardo

each of whom wanted to have a little chat; they arrived from back home, each with a new version of the same song, each with some souvenir so he wouldn't forget where he was from, each with cash.

Sent by the tyrant to offer them relief in exchange for a declaration of loyalty, after which they could return home and be at peace, with their families, with their loved ones, home is where the heart is: take it.

He refused. The others refused as well. But wasn't it disgraceful, then, to have accepted the money Margarita had sent, money earned from her job working at the little store? They needed that money to survive, Margarita and their daughters and their son. He hadn't even been present for the births of María de Jesús and Josefa. Hadn't been there to take care of them or witness their astonishment at the sun in the sky each day. But he'd taken their money to offset what Pepe had lost and to save up for their return, that's what he told himself. Now they had to scrabble to make the most of what was left, because they couldn't find a room with board in the third ward, and the first ward was for whites, and the old quadrant was impossible at the rock-bottom price they'd been paying. Borrego suggested taking a room overlooking a latrine.

He read in the local papers that they'd arrested two itinerant women who'd been singing without a permit. It was unclear whether they had been arrested for being women, for singing, for being itinerant, or all of the above. A carpenter accused the woman next door of running a house of ill repute, and then of trying to burn down his carpenter's shop when he complained. And the Plan of Ayutla was still in the news, ousting Santa Anna and calling an extraordinary congress; it had been wise to send Comonfort: they weren't on the sidelines now. There was no turning back.

He also read a story that confirmed what he'd been told in person that morning:

"You know," said the cop in insolent Spanish after emerging from the fog, ahead of his horse—not riding it, not leading it, just ahead of it. Twigs: that was the name he'd finally seen on the man's badge. "You know, yesterday some poor devil tripped not a block from where we stand now and was crushed by a coal car. Not from around here. Guy was Irish. Shocking how easy these foreigners die."

"And I," said Madame Doubard, "was in heaven. You see, I think heaven, the famous one, was also full of all manner of smells and all manner of animals, and that the men there too thought every single thing in existence should be grateful to them—ha. But it was still heaven. How could anyone bear

73

to leave such a decomposed place, when this is just the kind of place where things really happen? I should know: if you want to dance, you've got to lose all composure, acquire a taste for the ridiculous. That's how this city started out, or this version of the city, anyway: with no fear of the ridiculous."

Madame Doubard was seventy years old and had silver curls, glasses that bugged out her eyes, and a body that couldn't sit still even though the three of them—she, Pepe, and he—were sitting down for tea. Madame Doubard had been a chorus girl on the old continent, the rotten one.

"Before this city came to exist, in order for it to exist, we sent over the blind, which is what we Europeans always do: send the blind or half-blind, those who see only what they can grab or extract, so as not to waste time on whatever was there before them. That's when we begin. And this city began with sick people, prostitutes, thieves, drunks. France sent over whatever they didn't want. That was long ago, but some of us learned the habit of not being ashamed of that, of being detritus. Could there be any place more interesting than the one where all the chaff gets tossed? That's where new things ferment, where people learn to innovate, even if those who did the tossing refuse to see it."

They'd knocked on her door, and as soon as she opened it, Pepe had launched into the little speech he'd memorized: they were looking for a room, preferably with board; they didn't have much, but always paid on time. There was a decent chance that at least some of his words resembled English; she had listened to all of them with a friendly smile, then asked a question in Creole, which he responded to in book French, and then she asked Spanish? and they nodded eagerly.

"So you've come for the room. The rent is more than you say you have. But come in, come in, let's have a cup of tea and talk; whenever possible, I find new ways to not keep quiet."

She told them that she'd come over to sing at the Théâtre d'Orléans, "the old one, the one that burned down, so this was many years ago; I was even prettier than I am now." Then after that, she'd just stayed. As she was explaining why, Madame Doubard suddenly stopped and said:

"Wait, of course there's something I can offer you. Come."

They followed her. Through a living room with divans and a mannequin wearing too many hats and blouses, to the second floor, where there was an empty room with a bed, nightstand, armchair, and even a shelf full of books, which got their hopes up, but Madame Doubard didn't even break her stride; she continued down to the end of the hall, where she stopped and did a little leap in the air to pull on a cord, from which came a folding ladder. Come, she repeated, then climbed the ladder and said:

"It isn't a bedroom, strictly speaking. Strictly speaking, what it *is* is an attic." And here she raised a finger authoritatively. "But at least it *is*."

It was indeed an attic. But an attic in a stone house, impervious to hurricanes, and in the old quadrant to boot, close to their jobs. And it was all there was.

"How much?"

"Five. No board."

And that's how they ended up in the house on Saint Peter.

The green skin that lay over the city began to sprout white dots, as though afflicted by an outbreak that then quickly became an explosion, an explosion of five-armed pinwheels: jasmine flowers; jasmine everywhere, on the slightest pretext, an epiphany of the nose, one that upended all previous understanding of the city, like discovering that round was square or sweet was spicy or that what had merely been waiting, waiting, waiting could also be a distinct pleasure for the lungs, the victory of jasmine.

The other owner of the house on Saint Peter was named Polaris. She was a bundle of wild gray and white curls, wore a purple collar, and barked at anyone she heard going past the house; but after Madame Doubard opened the door, Polaris would prance around, studying the visitors, and then head off to a corner and eye them quietly.

It didn't take long for Polaris to accept that he and Pepe were no longer strangers, and she soon stopped eyeing them from her corner, though from time to time, for no apparent reason, she'd jump up and stand on alert in front of one of them, then in front of the other, give a little yip of warning, and then scratch or lick herself and forget about them.

When Madame Doubard wasn't looking, Polaris would hump Pepe's leg.

Another time, when no papers from home had arrived, he began an exhaustive read of the local paper, which reported nothing out of the ordinary: two bodies found bobbing by the riverbank, several people suspected of setting fire to their own and others' homes, people stabbing each other in the street, women sent to the House of Work for being uncivilized; he retained none of the details, or if he did, they vanished the second he got to a brief paragraph tacked onto the end of other news, which reported that there'd been an earthquake in Mexico, and the worst of it had hit Oaxaca.

"I couldn't find any either," said Santacilia, "not at the levee, not in the coffeeshops. It happens sometimes. Distribution problems: something happens at the port of exit, or on the boat while in transit, or they get stolen on arrival, and we go a few days with no outside news. But everything here is so intense, you forget other countries even exist."

"Not me," he said.

"Not you, forgive me. I hope your family is okay."

He'd written to find out, of course, but who knew when his letter would arrive, or when a reply would, and the newspapers apparently never would. First he'd gone to Cabañas, to no avail, now he'd come to Santacilia, also to no avail. Neither had any. Santacilia suggested they go for a walk, to take their minds off it. And so, to take their minds off it, he told him about the other cities where he'd been in exile—Seville, Gibraltar, New York—all of them rich, but none like this, where you could so clearly see the blood on the gold.

The streets became less crowded, the pockets of shade more so. They walked past a wiry man, very old and very black, who looked like nothing could surprise him, heading toward the lake; somehow he managed to balance a long cylindrical drum under one arm.

"Where do they play when there's no festivities?"

"All over: in secret, in abandoned houses, in some free man or free woman's rooms, in the city's nooks and crannies. They used to gather on Sundays to drum in an open field not far from here, just outside the old city."

"I walked by there one day. They don't play there anymore?"

"It was banned."

"What do they use it for now?"

Santacilia stopped short, then turned to give him a look of something like pity.

"You don't know?"

Some by the foot, in single-file, one after the other. Others by the hand. Still others shackled by the neck. Almost entirely naked.

One man with the face of an owner and another with the face of a fiend, captor and overseer, sauntered among the captured, mauling them, opening their mouths, asking questions of the trader.

Santacilia pointed to a group of captured. "Some of these folks don't tally the years by calendar, which most of them don't have, but by overseer. The most bloodthirsty are the most remembered, a mark in time."

A trader forced one of the captured to lift a boulder with both hands, then with one hand, then to lift the trader himself. Strong but docile, the man touted; plus, this one even knew how to pick cotton and cut cane.

"And if that's not enough," added the trader, speaking at a normal volume but leaning in as if confiding a secret, "the boy's green, born in Africa. Yes, I know, I know, but shhh . . . what's a dealer to do if a boat carrying a shipment from Africa accidentally sails off course? Hmm? Deny my customers the merchandise? No. Y'all rule the roost around here; there's a reason this market for hands is the biggest one in the country, and this country the best one in the world."

"Hands?"

"That's what they call them on the plantations."

Hands. Hands with no person. But, of course, each pair of hands had a person. They could convince themselves that what they were doing wasn't being done to a person if they called them hands. But hands come at the end of a person.

And they were chained. Here, of all places. They could have done it anywhere. But the owners had decided to do it here: here, where the captured used to gather in song; here, where they kept memory alive, where they were more than just hands, this was the place they decided to sell them like cattle.

At Gravier Market (the name stuck with him like a tic, a reminder of the presence of evil) people were kept in pens, sold in halls. One sign boasted Locally Owned! In some halls the traders stuck tools in their hands to demonstrate their trade: blacksmith, carpenter, bricklayer.

A man lay broken on the floor, moaning, almost imperceptibly stirring and then recollapsing, as if attempting to escape the touch of his shirt. He was being sold at a discount, since, having had the gumption to look at the master's daughter, the man had been whipped so bad he'd been rendered useless.

"But you could put him to work in the house, have him there as an example to the others."

The other horror at Gravier that stuck with him forever was seeing one man's jubilation. More pale than white, unshaven, unwashed, dowsed in filth, the man grasped a wad of cash as if it were the hand of providence as the trader presented a young, very young, woman, an adolescent, in fact: she was trained to work, of course, had done nothing else since birth, but now—just this week!—she'd become a woman, ready to reproduce. "Three for the price of one: worker, fertile, and—not for long—virgin! Who'll pay top dollar, who'll pay top dollar, don't be shy, don't be cheap, be wise, don't you see, this investment will pay for itself: you buy her and you'll never need to buy another; you can produce your own hands! Her children will be additional capital, as Founding Father Jefferson said. And if, after birthing all the hands you need, she can't give you any more, have no fear, you can free her and guess what, the offspring are still your property! It's a win-win."

Win-win, the trader said.

And the man, who was more pale than white, who looked like he might collapse at any second, seemed only to regain his composure with the help of the bills in his fingertips.

"I been waiting so long for an opportunity like this," the man said. "I've worked, I've saved, I do no one any harm: all I want's a fair shake, just one shot, a chance to leave some patrimony to my kin."

The auction began. Someone on the far side of the exchange was also bidding on the girl; on this side, people were rooting for the now-tearful man, transferring bills from one hand to the next as the bids increased, saying:

"One shot, this is my one shot."

The trader, between one bid and the next, kept repeating Win-win, win-win!

When the wretch had only one bill left to transfer to his other hand, his competitor on the other side of the exchange threw his hands up in defeat and the crowd cheered the victor, still crying, but now they were tears of joy; people patted his back, happy for him. Up on the block the girl stared at the ground with vacant eyes.

At the Hotel Saint Louis, one of the most luxurious, people were sold right there at the entrance, in the rotunda. Male captured were dressed in suits and even bowlers but were either shoeless or wearing shoes that clearly did not fit. Female captured were made up like the whitewashed and given parasols, as if to protect them from the sun, because fine folk need to be protected from the sun. The women were sold like baubles. Baubles that could be beaten if they didn't do as ordered.

Why bring me here, he asked himself, why, why, why on earth did he bring me to these places. But then immediately he wondered: How did I not see it myself.

Ocampo, seeing the penury in which he and Pepe sweated out their survival, wanted to split the cost of the attic with them or give them enough to rent the empty room as well, but they wouldn't allow it. Even between friends, free money is poisoned money. So Ocampo decided to move in himself, with his daughter Josefa, give her the bed while he slept on the floor, like Pepe (though there's floors, and there's floors: the one in the fancy room was covered with a thick rug; the one in the attic was covered only with dust), but said who knew how long he'd stay.

"I didn't think we'd be here in the summer, and I don't

81

know if Josefa can take it," Ocampo said. "Plus it's time to be getting back; it's all kicked off without us."

Newspapers from home had returned to the levee, but no matter how hard he shook them, there was no news of the earthquake victims.

The local papers reported a fire at a factory where they made camphene, used for celluloid, gunpowder, and the heart. A raging inferno. He'd seen it in the distance but assumed it was a ship. An editorial celebrated the government's poisoned-sausage plan but complained that they hadn't implemented another plan to pick up the corpses; consequently, there were dead dogs all over the city.

That was the day Polaris disappeared.

"Let me tell you something," the New Yorker said with the gleeful naivete of a man about to share a revelation, "the key to progress is not simply being able to put a new idea into practice but being able to see when that idea has grown stale."

Though he could understand almost everything by this point, it was still impossible for him to converse in English without each word feeling like a burden.

The New Yorker, who was redheaded, thin by design, and condescending without being insulting, had struck up a conversation with Ocampo about the progress of nations at the Hotel Conti.

"Don't get me wrong, there's whips and then there's whips: there's one, really impressive, that makes a very effective sound: crack. A miracle of engineering and simplicity. But the time for whips has passed. Things are changing. And folks down here know it too, that's why the plantation owners say they uphold the system not for the profit but because plantations are like big families; say they're protecting their hands from a world where they wouldn't know how to survive."

"Seems to me that appropriating the wages of one generation after another is pretty profitable."

"Oh, indeed it is. Us Yankees don't deny that. Southerners down here write us off, like we don't know what we were talking about. But we invented the South. We're the ones who came and bought all this from the French; we're the ones who imported over a million Africans. And that was vital to lay the foundation of wealth for this great nation. But what they're doing here . . . reproducing them, well, aside from being reprehensible, it's an unfair business advantage."

"What do you do? What brings you here?" he asked in glitchy English.

"Commodities agent. I deal in hands, large-scale."

"You . . . traffic humans."

"No, no, no, no." The New Yorker flapped his arms, waving them to purify the air. "I don't even lay eyes on them; people who do that live in a bygone era, all I do is close deals, the financial side; times are changing, but not overnight. And in the meantime, someone's got to meet market demand. The market never stops."

As the New Yorker spoke, a feather fluttered in a window or fled the kitchen and landed on his shoulder. The man went Hey to a passing waiter and with an eyebrow indicated his shoulder. The waiter whipped out a handkerchief and removed the feather. And that too was a horror: what have we lost when you can't shake off your own jacket or wash a single dish, when comfort is your only concern. What are we willing to ignore, or let atrophy, for the right to indolence. What a monstrous thing, comfort.

He had the urge to explain this to Mata and then realized that he was no longer there; Mata had gotten up and was out strolling with Josefa; in fact, only now did he realize that Mata, so combative, seemed suddenly to have lost interest in conspiring, and for days had been disappearing and reappearing with Josefa. He saw Ocampo eyeing them with the intense concentration of a watchmaker.

A few days later Ocampo and Arriaga announced they were headed to Brownsville, to roll out the Revolutionary Junta. No sooner had they done so than Mata announced he was going too. They would all go.

Walking past the cemetery, he saw a number of badges shoving a man. The man was cuffed, hands in front, yet somehow holding a small white coffin in his arms. They were carting him off for attempting to bury his child without a proper license. Where would they toss the child now? Into jail with the father? Some drawer in an office? A hallway? A garbage can? Would they leave the child out to rot in the sun?

You could feel the heat like a premonition, but this still wasn't the real deal.

"Oh, this ain't the worst," said Twigs, appearing behind him as if reading his mind. "This ain't but a taste. Wait till August. Wait till September. And wait'll you see what comes along with the heat: Yellow Jack."

Twigs laughed. His horse had kept going when Twigs stopped and now turned back to ask what the holdup was.

He said nothing in reply but fixed his eyes on the officer. It was a skill he had, being able to look in a way that showed no fear yet also no defiance.

"August," Twigs repeated. "Before August the city was insalubrious. A little worse than usual, but like usual. Come September, place turned into a veritable pustule. We ended up pretending to bury people but really just sprinkled dirt on them. Eight thousand dead. Can you feature that? Eight thousand. Some say more. Truth is, after the first thousand you stop counting. Yellow Jack . . . See you around, amigo."

Twigs didn't say friend, he said amigo: *uhmeego.*

He began walking again, and a minute later he could hear Twigs and his horse ambling along behind him.

Places sometimes invent themselves atop the bones of other places. To *them*, this city used to be the North; to that man it didn't used to be anything, and now it was the South, as well as the border with the east. And that border had to be expanded, because without plantations, there was no civilization.

He read in the news about the Kansas-Nebraska Act, which said that anywhere without an express prohibition against it, it was legal to capture people (possess, it said), and that even if a captor traveled to federal territory with his captives, that didn't make them free; the captured had the law branded on their skin.

He read that Gadsden was in negotiations for the railway from Louisiana to California to end at a camp for the captured, on the Mexican side.

He read that France and England were planning to turn the electric telegraph into a speaking telegraph, placing metal plates above and below the tongue and then connecting them to a cable that could transmit words. It had already been tested, with successful results. Successful results. Did that not depend on what was said?

Another story warned of the dangers of the heat wave and recommended placing a damp handkerchief under one's hat; if the hat is very thick, make holes in it.

And the others moved out of limbo. To Brownsville, where they felt like they were actually doing something. Here they'd grown tired of being anyluckers, anylucking from a distance: such and such'll happen with anyluck, this or that with anyluck, anyluck with anyluck. There, at least they were technically closer. That's why they went.

Or else they were fleeing the hot.

Or else they were sick of all the dead strangers.

Or else because Brownsville was a place they could discuss matters; and everything remained to be discussed.

He and Pepe stayed put in the limbo they knew.

Margarita sent a letter saying everyone was fine, giving them a few days of good cheer.

Then began the season of vomiting.

FIVE

From the first eternity they'd already spent in the city they progressed to the second, far longer and more eternal eternity of the summer. Summer changes everything: the purpose of the night, the awareness of one's body. Time expands, like when you're a child and each day is endless. A childhood sun, not passing through but instead taking great pains to beat down on the city.

At the very start of summer, just before those first days when the heat becomes the hot, Borrego hands him a small vial of crystalline liquid and says:

"I'm leaving town till autumn at least. I don't know when I'll be back, so just take this and put it in the coolest spot in your house. And may you never need to use it."

"What is it?"

"Quinine."

He searches for Polaris methodically: first circling the block where the house sits, then fanning out to neighboring blocks; next he traverses Saint Peter down to the river, then to the vegetable market; methodically, anything can be done as long as you do it methodically, proceed with logic. But what does he know of dog-logic? It's unknowable. He'd need to learn the language dogs use when they speak to each other in silence. So he tries to walk as if sniffing, curious; he lets himself be startled by a carriage, and after that simply trots along without caring where. Doggedly, he checks alleyways, potholes, and empty lots, anxious but focused. He skirts a stiff corpse on one corner. Not Polaris.

In the brief interim between the heat and the hot, when the streets are dotted with buttons of jasmine and all other smells are vanquished, souls are at peace, flocks of birds appear in the mornings to practice their language skills, as if all of them were polyglots. For a few days, which in the second eternity, the one on its way, are but an instant, it's easy to believe things will be this way forever: the air, the things, and the senses in perfect harmony.

Later, any illusion that the swamp's elements are under control disappears. It starts slow, almost imperceptible: paving stones still warm at night, water no longer cool though still refreshing, unlike when the real hot arrives.

The real hot arrives slowly but not subtly, and by the time you can say its name it's already named itself, littering the streets with sunstroked folk. The sunstroked die trusting their brains, and their brains betray them: suddenly they stop, attempt to grab hold of a pole that isn't there, and bite the dust, dead of cosmic death. He's seen it.

The canal is covered in a slick of green that makes it indistinguishable from the street, and sometimes people fall in and sometimes they never reappear; almost always it's visitors, which means it matters less. But one day he sees someone who looks like the man from his first day and follows him at a distance; the man speeds along, seeming to suspect he's being tailed; he tries to get closer to see if the blotch on his back is the image that would confirm it is who he thinks it is, but the man appears to sense something—not *him*—looks in all directions, then picks up the pace, passes a wall of men by the green slime canal, and there comes a splash. Rushing to the wall, he peers over the edge but can't see the man anywhere, only a slight undulation in the boggy canal.

It's not like there's a drop in holdups or weapons are put away, or like the hot evinces some new virtue in folks in general or in any observable manner, unless quiet desperation is a virtue, but at a certain time of day it does yield a new attitude: the solidarity shared by those who've survived a common enemy and gather to celebrate their feat. Nights are filled with confabulation, crowdeder than ever, not in festivity but in relief.

On one of these nights he stops in to see Cabañas and, as Cabañas prepares to lock up, he looks at the stacks of ads he used to deliver; he stands before a towering pile of posters.

"Are you delivering these today?"

"No, it's too late now. Tomorrow."

Discreetly he pulls one from the pile and takes it for himself.

After accompanying Cabañas for a few blocks, he says goodbye, but rather than head to the house on Saint Peter, he crosses the old quadrant and goes to the vegetable market.

He sees Thisbee working and singing, pouring coffee and joshing, thissing and thatting in the blessedly kind-of-cool night. He signals Come; she waves back but doesn't stop thatting; he signals again in what's clearly not a hey-there but a come-here, fingertips and all, and she replies as if it were a game. Then he slaps his thigh, which sparks mirth as well as curiosity, so she approaches, and the moment she's there before him he grabs her arm; Thisbee is shocked not only because he's never touched her before but also because the second he does so he lets her arm go and furtively slips her a poster that says **WANTED** and features not a face but a tattoo identifying Serge's still-at-large killer, identical to Thisbee's tattoo, now hidden by the poster. At the same time he sees that up her sleeve, Thisbee has a double-edged knife.

Borrego hasn't returned, and even though they've got his keys, sometimes they stay in the attic and attempt to breathe the thick and suffocating air of summer. There at the edge of monotony, the composition of dust, light, and time is revealed.

He can see the corpuscles that light is made of, the ones Newton spoke of, traveling swiftly, hurtling themselves through the window. But Newton claimed corpuscles traveled in straight lines, and he can see this light do its own thing, can see that as soon as it enters the room it gets groggy and settles down with the dust.

And time goes muzzy too. They stare and stare, and in the interminable hours find new spots on the wall, new bugs staking their claim, the changing textures of the wood, the way it swells in the hot. They stare and stare and think the day is done and then look through the shutter slats and see it's only midday. When the suffocating air becomes unbreathable they're forced to roll the dice outdoors.

"I want to go home."

Who said that? Him or Pepe? They both think it. Go. No

stopping on the way. No planning. Just go. Go now. Sit in shade that's truly cool.

Every day gets hotter.

Every day more people hunch over in the street as if their spines can no longer hold them up.

Every day they see more mouths exploding with bloody gums.

Every day there are more dead.

One hundred twenty-two.

Two hundred seven.

Two hundred twelve.

Two hundred twenty-eight.

Three hundred ninety-three.

Four hundred eighty-four.

Five hundred thirty.

It's impossible to see when, or how, to get home before becoming a number himself.

Madame Doubard is off.

She calls them to the salon, offering tea and cookies. She sits, hands between her knees. She looks as if her bones have turned to wire.

"I'm not the leaving kind," she says, looking them in the eyes as she speaks, "but I can't stay here any longer. For the first time, I feel this place pushing me out. I'm no delicate flower. I've buried plenty of folks, oh, have I ever. Folks who were my blood and folks who were my heart. But this, my only companion, gone . . . With *that* out there . . . She could be rotting right around the corner for all I know. I know you've both searched for her too. What more can we do? What more can I do?"

She takes a set of keys from a dresser, hands it to them.

"Take the room Mr. Ocampo and his daughter were in, there's an extra cot in there. No need to carry on suffering up in the attic. I'll tell you where to post the rent. Should you decide to leave, send word. And lock the place up tight."

Madame Doubard gets up and walks to the door. They help load her trunks onto a carriage.

"We'll keep looking," he says.

Madame Doubard blesses them with lips and hands, and leaves.

Ice. Brought in from Norway, they say, or New England. One of those places with a halfbaked sun. But where was that water before it got frozen and sliced and stuck on a ship? What memory does that water have? What other river ended up in those parched bodies?

He walks to where the ice wagon has stationed itself, carrying a leather pouch and a couple of coins, to see how much he can get. A dozen people cluster, too anxious to form a line and too torrid to fight over it, just sweating and raising their hands. From within the gaggle, someone shouts:

"Anybody got the fever, you can't be here!"

They all look at each other a second, as if they could see the sickness, then keep begging.

No one knows how it spreads. Some say it's the heat. Others say it's the swamp. Others that it's foreigners, that they've got to stop letting them into the city.

"I'm creole," says one guy, "it doesn't scare me. We creoles are acclimatized."

The man is whitewashed, dressed up as if off to the opera. No one lets him through, if that's what he was hoping for. He's the most prosperous-looking of the customers. The rest are clearly here to buy ice for others, for the house where they serve or the brothel where they work; he recognizes a few waiters from the coffeeshops. The whitewashed guy flaps his hands in anger. No: he's shooing a squad of mosquitoes that have stopped to devour his neck.

Then he too feels a bite on his face and slaps the bug away.

The icemen are bewilderingly bundled in sweaters and scarves, unloading blocks from the back of the wagon, where the ice is stacked like see-through walls; one boy takes people's money and another behind him slices off chunks of ice and hands them over. When it's his turn and he takes out his money and picayune sack, the boy makes a Don't waste my time face, picks a few fallen pieces of ice, slips them into the sack, and waves a hand that says Scram.

Walking away, he revels for a second in the cold of the sack against his chest, then nearly drops it in shock—catches it midair—seeing her there, sniffing the cool of the wagon with a pack of dogs: Polaris. She's covered in filth, but he can still see her collar and tag, and she looks livelier than ever.

"Polaris!" he cries.

Polaris turns in shock, pricks her ears, and leaps and bounds toward him; he could swear she's smiling, then she jumps at his knees, wags her tail, sneezes. The other dogs look on for a moment before turning their attention back to the ice. He scrubs his fingers through her grimy coat and says:

"Come, Polaris, let's go! You coming? Come. You coming?"

Polaris comes, and to keep the treasure in his free arm from falling, he heads back with both blessings to Saint Peter.

People go through the day sledgehammered by the sun, until at some point they can no longer hold it all in and do what they must to keep from going mad, or to exercise their madness, why not.

Waiting for Thisbee at the market, he hears:

That some rowdies were arrested for downing tools on a ship's deck and refusing to work without a raise; they were accused of rioting, though clearly they're strikers even if nobody uses that word here: saying *strike*, in this country, is forbidden. That a fisherman grabbed his dagger and stabbed an officer in the chest after being fined for the fifth time for selling bad fish. That two engineers on a steamer got in a knife fight over a woman. That a powder keg was found on Canal, on neutral ground, as if anyone needed more fire. That two hundred firefighters showed up outside the jail to demand that one of their men be freed, bringing a band along to play, and when the cops came out to disperse them, all but the drummer fled. That a three-day-old infant was abandoned on a windowsill. That a two-month-old baby died of convulsions caused by the fear the mother passed on in her milk, terrified at the idea of the father returning. And that one man bit off the lip of another.

He hears more and more, anylucking Thisbee's appearance, but no matter how many tales he hangs around for, she doesn't turn up, and he decides to return to Saint Peter.

On the way back, he runs right into her. It takes a few seconds for him to recognize Thisbee, because she's sheathed in a bright yellow dress that covers her hands and half her face as well. Then he remembers he's been dreaming of her like this, as she is now, in a way he won't allow himself to do when awake. The gut knows things of which the waking mind is ignorant.

He also sees that she's giddy in a way he recognizes. Aha. He'd been about to ask why she wasn't at the market, but. Aha. Instead he says:

"The tales I heard today."

"Well, don't go turning into one," she replies. "If you've no need to go out, hole up and keep yourself to yourself during the day. By the way, where are you holing up?"

He asks her to come see the house on Saint Peter. On the way, he tells her about Madame Doubard, about how the others are gone and it's only him and Pepe now; about Polaris, and who she is and how she got lost and how he found her without a care amid all the loss of man and dog life. And Thisbee says Atta girl.

They can hear Polaris and her prancy-paws, anxious on the other side of the door; she doesn't bark, knowing it's him, but once the door is open she ignores him and instead circles Thisbee, dancing around, trotting out a tug-rag, and begging her to play. And Thisbee does, while taking stock of the luxuries all around, less in admiration than to prove to herself just how much furniture and gilded crap gets stockpiled by the rich.

Pepe's not there. He shows Thisbee where they sleep. Almost as nice as my place, she says, then looks him in the eye, smiles, and he feels his skin slough off in embarrassment.

"Don't go getting any ideas," she says.

They come to the courtyard, which has a pond with a reflecting pool, where he's stashed the vial of quinine. Thisbee touches three fingers to it, fascinated now; she knows what it is but has never seen it. Then she turns and says Take care. And heads back to her own environs.

Yellow Jack comes on like something else, like a summer chill, like a shudder or a change in air pressure, over and over. It's not the fever, no: it's the heebie-jeebies, it's the lack of water, it's the lack of shade. Then comes the cough. A dainty little cough, repeated over and over. He goes out in search of medicine, at the corner comes across a man spewing black vomit. He buys orange blossom, surely that'll make it pass, surely, surely, surely, it'll pass.

It doesn't pass. The next morning, on waking, he sees Pepe's skin all yellowy. He runs to the mirror but already knows what he'll see, because he can feel his body desiccating from the inside out.

He goes back to bed to lie down for a minute, just a minute, any second now he'll find the strength to stand up and go get the quinine, any minute.

He wakes up who knows how much later. Polaris is beside him, between the bed and the cot, where Pepe has not so much as shifted. Polaris stands, looks at him for a second, and ambles out of the room.

He feels yellow inside. Yellow guts, yellow bones, his blood transubstantiating into pus. He has to get up; nobody's coming to help. He lifts his head a few inches but it immediately falls back onto the pillow. Closes his eyes to make a more concerted effort, but that's when the dreams begin.

BENITO'S FIRST DREAM
THE ELEMENTS

He's back in the enchanted lagoon, floating face up; the raft can't decide whether to sink or float. There is no moon, there are no stars, the sky is heavy, it propagates; he can feel it pressing down on his nose, to the point of crushing him, the point, the point, the point, an emptiness lurking there, lying in wait, suspended, never actually falling. No need to fall. Because the oppression is actually inside his body. The elements are inside his body, and no one can help him.

He discovers a pendulum by his side: five steel balls, each suspended by two diagonal cables, each of which is attached to two rails. He can see his reflection in the balls. The scar on his forehead looks bigger than it is.

He reaches out and lifts one of the balls. It seems to leave a trace in the air, a trace that, on closer inspection, is in fact the mathematical formula for curvilinear motion. He lets go of the ball, it drops, and on striking the one beside it, which had been at rest, multiple equations explode from the balls, denoting the force one transmits to the next, and that the one after that transmits to the adjacent one, the identical resistance they exert, momentum.

He's no longer alone, the pendulum is explaining to him the universe.

Suddenly formulas begin multiplying all around the pendulum. Describing the movement of his hand as he pulls it away, describing his scrawny body, describing the flimsy, wet raft. Then they start building: they collide at a vertex which they themselves have created through perpendicular force, they create the tension in a wall that exists only by dint of what they express, and then another wall and another vertex and another wall and another vertex and another wall and a roof, all built by another tongue, blessed math, a tongue he knows, building him a shelter from the elements. It's exact and precise, this shelter, built of numbers and letters and gradients and integrals . . . which collapse around him like tiny branches.

Then something changes. The equations describe what they're doing, autopoietically, they bend a board on the raft and describe the crack it creates, stack another board on top and describe the gravitational force one exerts upon the other; a lone bird flies overhead and the equations, as though they had arms, describe themselves ascending to it and trapping it and gutting it and using its remains to fortify this precise little shelter they've built him, for which more material is required, but there isn't enough, only that which he wears, his thread-bare suit, his dusty shoes. They're using it all. He knows that he is next, that he is now the only remaining material, that the shelter must now be made not for him, but of him.

Extending a hand, he stops the pendulum, but the mono-logue of reason no longer needs him, and rather than stop, it surrounds him, geometrizes him, and begins to detach his hands.

His eyes fly open. He's in the house on Saint Peter. Still feel-ing yellow. Pepe is lying there beside him, asleep but no longer corpse-like, his body jerking slightly, giving little tremors, which means he's better than he was . . . when? . . . Polaris is again sitting between them, on the alert.

Like the last time he awoke, Polaris gives him a look and then stands, but this time she hurtles out of the room. He hears her bark.

The energy that allowed him to wake begins to abandon him. He starts to let go, but before he's carried off he sees someone in the doorway. He recognizes the figure, despite the white dress that covers her. Thisbee. Nobody fills space the way Thisbee does. But he's still sinking, retreating back into his bones. Is it Thisbee? He sees her approach, her gloved hands open his mouth, he sees a dropper, feels the drops on his tongue. He lacks the strength to close his mouth. He watches Thisbee—is it Thisbee?—repeat the operation with Pepe. Watches her wrap the vial of quinine in a white handkerchief and tuck it away. Then he begins to dream again.

BENITO'S SECOND DREAM
MELCHOR OCAMPO: SOCIALIST VAMPIRE SLAYER

The parlor has the highest ceilings Ocampo has ever seen, and they're clean, with no cobwebs, as if inhabited. Black velvet curtains hang over the enormous picture windows. Lit candelabra protrude from the walls, sit on the dining room table, on several other tables. Two full-length portraits depict the hosts with discomfiting fidelity, as if they'd been done that very day, though it's evident the paintings are quite old.

The wine is excellent. So dark it's almost black.

"Aged one hundred years," says she, the marquess, milk-white breasts straining at her low neckline, "in French oak."

"American oak is also quite good." The marquis strokes his long mustache. "That's why we're in Louisiana. These oaks are like a rejuvenating cave."

They'd asked him to arrive at midnight. Said how much they'd heard about him, how happy they were that he had accepted the invitation. They serve him a steak that's practically raw and a salad of potatoes. Ocampo takes a very long time to finish, and when he does he asks for more. Neither of them are eating, but he doesn't ask why. He knows why. Knows what they are.

And they know what he is too.

"Tell us about how you shut down all the churches in your land, in . . . how do you say it?" the marquess asks.

"Michoacán. When I was governor. Not much to tell." He brushes it off with a wave of the hand. "I had no choice. They wanted to wrestle, so wrestle we did. Sometimes brute force is the only option."

"Amen," says the marquis, and both of them laugh, as if they've played a prank.

He excuses himself to go to the bathroom and on his way corroborates the information he's been given: a family— woman, man, two daughters—is being held prisoner in the kitchen. When they see him walk by, they shrink back and then embrace. There are wounds on their necks. Ocampo puts a finger to his lips not to request silence, since they're not making any noise, but to communicate complicity. He lingers in the bathroom before returning to the table.

The wine is gone; Ocampo waggles the bottle needlessly to call attention to the fact. The marquess says I'll get more, then stands and disappears down a hallway.

Ocampo takes this opportunity to stand as well. Now's the time. He walks over to a wall and says:

"Is this a water stain, or did the stone already look like this?"

The marquis stands, intrigued.

"Where?"

"Here, look." Ocampo points to a spot, and the marquis leans in to inspect it, resting his hand on the wall by the imaginary stain.

"I don't . . ."

His sentence goes unfinished. From a coat pocket, Ocampo whips out one of the fat rusty nails that have been weighing him down, from another he extracts the small hammer he brought expressly for this purpose, and before the marquis can fathom that this is all a trap, he nails the vampire's hand to the wall with one swift blow. The marquis turns to eye him in surprise, but Ocampo has pulled out the second nail and now pounds it through his other hand till it penetrates the wall. The marquis lets out a howl and bares his fangs; the whites of his eyes fill with blood.

The marquess has now returned to the parlor. She gapes, attempting to work out what is happening. It takes but a second. They've brought the enemy into their home. She roars and drops the bottle, which crashes to the floor without breaking, then in a single horrifying leap she flies across the parlor to pounce on Ocampo, fangs out, her fingernails suddenly long. Ocampo takes advantage of her momentum to hurl the marquess against a chair, which shatters. She recovers and slaps his face: a backhander; Ocampo feels a molar come loose, whips out a head of garlic, almost in triumph, but the marquess smacks his hand and sends it flying. Ocampo retreats, falls onto his back, and immediately she pounces again, kneeing him between the legs. He can't wrest her off, she's too strong, the best he can do is wedge an arm between his neck and the vampire's fangs. Using the other hand, he pulls out the dagger hidden with the remaining nails and plunges it into her heart. There's a brief reprieve from her onslaught as she sits on the floor and gazes in shock, almost offended at the dagger that now impales her to its hilt. Ocampo takes his chance to scuttle backward and stand. The marquess extracts the dagger with a swift yank. Now she's *really* pissed. Ocampo thinks perhaps he could have planned this better.

The marquis hasn't stopped howling all this time, but the nails are holding. The marquess turns to him; Ocampo knows she's going to free the marquis, knows he won't have another chance. They both leap, and the moment her palm lands on the wall to extract the nails, he pulls out one more and hammers it into her hand. Both vampires look on, incredulous, and that fraction of a second is all he needs to ram the final nail into the fourth and final vampire hand.

Ocampo falls to the ground a few feet back. He's exhausted, the arm he used to defend himself bleeding profusely. It seems as though all is silent for a few seconds. Then the howling of the vampires brings him back to reality. He approaches, hammer in hand, to clinch the nails. They attempt to bite him but cannot reach.

Ocampo picks the wine bottle up off the floor, opens it, takes a swig, and plops down in a chair.

"How? How? How is this possible?" roars the marquis, Ocampo unsure whether to him or to the marquess.

"What?"

"Those nails! How did you get holy nails into this house without our knowledge?"

"Ha!" Ocampo regards them in amusement.

"Why are you doing this?" Now it is she who roars. "You're not even religious!"

Ocampo takes another swig, stands.

"Look, madam, look, sir, I'm saying *madam* and *sir* because the time has come to acknowledge that no one is invulnerable just because they've got a noble title. Madam, sir: you can believe whatever you like, the Pope can believe whatever he likes. But this"—he points toward the kitchen—"this is not about beliefs. This is about the two of you being straight-up motherfuckers." Another slug from the bottle, and then he adds, "As is the Pope."

He walks to a window. The vampires thrash against the wall, juddering, screeching, their jaws snapping uselessly, biting the air.

"Crazy how long summer days are in this city, don't you agree? Sunrise comes earlier each day."

He grabs one end of the curtain decisively. Pauses. Turns to face them. And then says:

"I found those nails by the railroad tracks. Those aren't holy nails. They're workers' nails."

And with that he wrenches open the curtain.

SIX

He was seeing with the body of the saved and wondering, as if he'd only just arrived, What am I doing here, shocked at the streets he'd so often traversed. Nothing rewonders the world like the eyes of the saved: their rickety bones, their sallow flesh, their parched lips.

He saw the detail on the balcony of one of those strange houses: a humble design, but wrought in iron, even all the way up there. Pepe, who was also ghost-floating more than walking, paused and turned back to look at him like a newborn, but a grown and upright one, as if he'd been born of the sidewalk.

On the inside, however, he'd emerged from his stupor. He was wide awake, knew what it was he was seeing, and needed to see it up close. He started crossing the street, stopped in the middle of the intersection.

"Which side do you think the entrance is on?"

More than process the question, Pepe picked up on his incongruous energy, which had materialized as if by magic.

"Must be this one." He decided on Royal.

This was not the first time he'd crossed a threshold without asking. He turned the knob and walked in. Pepe holymothered behind him but tagged along regardless.

A cube of darkness. Immediately, a staircase. Beside that a hallway with a vertical shaft of light at the far end that brought—yes, the light—the sound of chirping from an inner courtyard. He ached to see it but was distracted no more than a second. He ascended the stairs as if the rug-covered steps themselves were urging him onward. Pepe, behind him, climbed up in heroic silence.

Two steps from the top of the staircase, a woman appeared before them. She stared at them in incredulity more than in fear, as if indignant at being forced to see something where normally there was nothing. This was the owner. You could tell by her face, all authority, that she was about to inform them that this was not the entrance for the help, or to ask if so-and-so had sent them, but in a stroke of inspiration he spoke first, raising an index finger with the solemnity of a child repeating his lessons:

"There are things that cannot be seen until the thing itself so decides."

And he scurried past her toward the balcony.

Pepe mumbled You're going to get us killed, then gave the owner a smile that said No trouble at all, ma'am, just doing our job. The owner turned to the balcony, then back to Pepe, attempting to figure out who they were, because clearly they weren't thieves, so perhaps she'd forgotten some builders were coming? *Shocking*, men of their ilk traipsing in with such impudence, and not even armed.

He approached the balcony, crouching lower with each

step, till one knee was on the floor and the design before his eyes. Yes: it was the same image he'd last seen on the skin of a drowned man.

The following months shot past like they'd escaped from a pressure cooker.

In November, he learned that in New Orleans the season of bliss was not spring but fall. The despotic sun picked up sticks, meaning people could be outside without cursing the elements. Sidewalks were once again inhabited; cotton, which had disappeared months ago, began to reappear at the levee; the loss of life went on, but it became unobtrusively endemic. Once more people whistled as they walked, opera season opened with Donizetti's *La favorite* at the Théâtre d'Orléans, and theater season opened at the Saint Charles with *Rob Roy MacGregor*, based on a Walter Scott novel. As if the city hadn't been sizzling only a few weeks ago.

Only a few weeks ago, there had been an infamous case involving a young woman who'd poisoned herself with strychnine, leaving behind a letter that instructed what should be done with her body but no explanation for her act. And there'd been pitched battles between militants from the American Party—the Know Nothings—and Irish immigrants, who they accused of being dirty, of being thieves, of coming to steal their jobs. Threats, injuries, fatalities. But who remembered any of that when you could breathe again.

As a boy, Santacilia had undoubtedly been a proper little man, always freshly bathed, elegant, spine as straight as the stem of

107

a spikenard. As an adult, his rectitude could be seen not only in his backbone but in the scientific clarity with which he approached any problem.

"So the revolution is a go?" asked Santacilia on the way to another coffeeshop he wanted him to see. "I've read contradictory reports in the papers, some saying Álvarez is in hiding, some that Santa Anna's already defeated."

"One can't rely exclusively on the papers. I regularly get reports by correspondence: Álvarez is not in hiding, nor has Santa Anna been defeated. The revolution is advancing not just in Guerrero but in Michoacán and Tamaulipas too."

"So it's in full swing . . . without you."

"Come again?"

"*They* are at the border and *you* are here, conspiring."

"One does not conspire for the sake of conspiring. It's imperative to prepare for what will come afterward."

They'd arrived. Santacilia paused before entering.

"That's all well and good. But the way I see it, one must know the difference between taking measure of the situation and being on the fringe of the situation. Or, worse, on the fringe of another's coattails. Come."

They entered. Before them were a number of long tables full of people deep in discussion, some sitting, others standing. On smaller, square tables were the day's papers, books, and ship manifests reporting arrivals and departures as well as merchandise on board. He heard a great deal of Creole and saw a great number of creoles, and more customers of varying negritude than at other coffeeshops.

"You've been to coffeeshops that are taverns, and maybe seen others called shebeens, which are like brothels that might or might not sell sex—though that's not what matters most, what matters is that they're clandestine, we'll go to one later—but this one here is like the one where you and I met."

"They sell no alcohol?"

"No, to avoid false pretexts: what they deal in here is more dangerous."

Santacilia pointed to a corner where a woman was teaching the alphabet to three black children of various ages.

"This is what scares them. Not booze. Oppressed and drunk is oppressed and docile. They only prohibit the sale of alcohol to certain groups of people, because if, on top of harassing them, you can make a quick buck from kickbacks—why not?"

They approached one of the long tables, where Santacilia slipped into the discussion like it was just his size. There were four or five young men, one young woman, and one young man dressed as a woman; though it wasn't Carnival, nobody seemed to be concerned. At times it almost appeared they were fighting, given all the body that went into their words, but then everyone would listen as the young woman spoke, sometimes in English, sometimes in Creole, both flecked with specks of still other tongues:

Yesterday they arrested three women at a coffeehouse on Phillipa, anyone see that? For drinking and obscene language, Some of us use obscene language even without speaking, interjected the man as woman, They arrested Ned too, said another, he's not free but he was living on his own with a white woman; she got sent to the workhouse for six months, And what about him? Nobody knows, the story only said he'll be punished appropriately. Everyone fell silent. Then someone said: We need to burn it all down, We need to haul out, said someone else, Ha, and go where? Up north, or to Mexico, We're not going anywhere, we're staying right here to beat them at their own game, using their rules, That makes no sense, the rules were made for them to win, But we're already winning in a way, aren't we? I mean, here we are, thinking aloud, Yeah, but thinking with *their* words, are you forgetting that people who traffic other people are called *brokers*?, with words like that you think we'll ever get ahead? wearing clothes like theirs, you think we'll ever get ahead? we have fewer rights each day, in case you haven't noticed, Yes, I have noticed, and yes, we're going to win, even if that's the way we do it, because we have no other choice, so we'll create our own rights, like Lanusse, who started a school for orphan girls of color, Wonder how long that'll last, or what they'll use it for, Do you know Tyler, the Texas slaver, has a plantation he calls Sherwood Forest, like he's Robin Hood, Shameless, Well, we'll call it by whatever name it deserves, under our breath if we have to, but that's how you start.

"Ah, youth," he heard someone say behind him. "Every generation rediscovers the wheel . . . Bless them."

A darker-skinned man, wearily athletic, hair sprinkled with gray, sat a few feet behind him.

"Good thing they're drinking coffee," the man added, looking at him now. "Coffee helps you think."

The man sipped his own drink, which was not coffee.

"You don't get involved?" he asked.

"I come here to listen. Not cause I got something to say, just cause it's beautiful to hear these kids doing something besides obey orders. But since you asked, I don't think we should pull up stakes, nor do I think whitey up north is going to come save us. We've got to survive any way we can. And being alive is already winning, the way I see it."

He was about to ask the man's name, when a boy poked his head in the door and shouted:

"Twigs!"

A second later, some secret operation was set in motion: the woman with the children slipped into a back room, and when the man as woman followed and the door opened again, he caught sight of other women too, including Thisbee, who noticed him but continued helping other people in and then shut the door.

A raid. Twigs walked in, followed by three badges. They shoved the darker-skinned men up against the wall and began frisking them and shouting. The man he'd been speaking to had slipped away who knows how. Suddenly Twigs stopped before him.

"What d'we have here? Been a while since I seen you, and look where you turn out to be. Must be trying to get yourself killed."

Twigs looked him up and down without another word, then opened the door the women had slipped through, but there was no one there. They arrested one black man and left.

That was what he learned in December.

The perfect weather lasted as long as the whisper of all things perfect, like dragonflies, and in January the cold sent folks back inside their houses, less out of inclemency than out of habit.

He used his time to answer correspondence. To Margarita

he said he was healthy and forever wondering what they were up to, she and the children. To Ocampo, that in New York Arrioja had dipped into his own pocket to procure four thousand rifles, artillery, munitions, and gunpowder; that Comonfort was already in Guerrero, and that soon he'd send those plants he'd requested (the man was prepared for war, but wherever he went, Ocampo planted flowers).

While he wrote, Polaris trotted her toys in one by one and placed them beside him, a rope, a ball, an old tug-rag—her own unfinished business—alternating between them. Only then did he remember the one letter he hadn't written.

"Madame Doubard!" He smacked his head. Immediately he began scribbling that Polaris was back and safe and playing, that they were fine and the house was fine, just a few lines so as to avoid any further delay. He slipped the letter into an envelope and set out to mail it. And on his way back discovered what January had to teach him.

He saw the sinewy man from the coffeeshop and waved, but the man did not respond, so he followed. The man was in no rush but stepped lightly. He caught up to him outside a smithy.

"Remember me? From the coffeeshop? We were talking and suddenly you were gone."

He introduced himself.

"Paul," the man replied, holding out a hand, suspicious but smiling. "I was gone, yessir, the black man knows when the best tête-à-tête is, in fact, a leg-à-leg."

"I was interested in what you were saying."

"Good, good, good, shows you know how to listen. That's good."

Paul appeared to be searching for a tool. He gripped a hammer.

"Is that what you do? Are you a blacksmith?"

"Yessir. One of the best."

"So you're an artist."

"I make what people ask for, and if they don't know what to ask for, I invent it. But the one who can really draw is my assistant. We specialize in balconies."

Balconies. He looked around, but there was no pen or paper in sight, so he crouched down and drew in the dirt.

"Have you ever seen something like this?"

Paul glanced at the drawing as if under obligation, already shaking his head, not really looking.

"Nope. Never seen that."

"Do you know anyone who . . . ?"

"Listen, since you're a man who knows how to listen: I know what I know, and I don't know what I don't know. And this, I don't know. Now let me get to work."

"Forgive me," he said, and then stood, brushed the dirt from his knees, and walked off.

The man didn't look the way Pepe had so keenly promised he would back in February: like something you've never seen, but not like the drunken ruckus of the holy days—parades, firecrackers, debauchery. You've got to see him. But he didn't see him, or he did, but all he saw was the man in question, immobile, just standing there in the bayou, legs spread wide, watching for the water to whiffle.

Suddenly the man grew more still but no more stiff, and kind of dissolved, no longer a man in the swamp but an element of the swamp; softly, almost imperceptibly, from between his legs peeked the scuted snout of a gator and, in the man's hand, the glint of a machete that flew up, then plunged down, with a crack, into the animal's head. For a fraction of a second, the gator thrashed in the water and then toppled onto itself as if from a great height. The man stood there a moment, both hands on the machete's grip; then he heaved it out, rinsed it off, hurled it ashore, and slipped his hands skillfully, tenderly, under the gator's head. He turned to the two of them, whose presence he had yet to acknowledge, and said to Pepe:

"Grab him by the tail: we're going to pull him out."

He helped too. The gator was only medium-sized—a meter, meter and a half long—but heavy, so heavy. They lugged it back to a table by the shore, and with a very sharp knife the man began to skin it as he spoke. First he made an incision in one foot, then introduced a hollow reed and began to blow and blow till the gator inflated. He sealed the tip of the reed with mud and left it there. Next he sliced all down the animal's back and legs, and carefully began lifting away the skin so as not to tear it.

"Pepe says you two were sick."

"We were. You didn't catch it?"

"No."

"How'd you manage that?"

"We no longer live in the city. We go there for business, but not during those months."

We was a group of Houma, Pepe had told him, who traded skins and acted as interpreters. This man spoke an imperial sort of Spanish, vees and zees banged up by use.

"You're not white." The man pointed at him with his knife. "Where are your people from?"

"Oaxaca," he replied, pointing behind him as though Oaxaca were right back yonder. "Mexico. What about yours?"

"From here," the man said. "Bulbancha."

"Is that the name of this place?"

"That's the name of this place."

"But didn't the Europeans destroy what it used to be?"

"A name tells many things. If one of the things it tells is the name of a destruction, then that's what it says, on top of everything it was already saying."

The man flipped the gator and began slicing it along the jawline and then down the belly. A woman approached with buckets, gave the man a few orders in Houma, and walked away without looking at them.

"Place of many tongues, that's what it means: Bulbancha. We'd been trading long before the others arrived. They call us savages now, but they were the ones who knew nothing. What to eat, how to heal themselves, how to build; they didn't understand the water . . ." He stopped a minute and looked at them. "Who on earth would grid a swamp? We should've let them drown but instead we helped them, and look what good that did.

Until a few years ago the mayor would still receive us, they'd hold ceremonies, give us gifts—you know, for our loyalty. Not anymore. And it's not because we're not loyal now: it's because we're in the way."

Finally he'd removed the entire skin except for the head and feet, exposing the pink-and-white flesh of the gator, which was no longer a gator but the prototype of a monster. The man began slicing off long strips of flesh and tossing them into the buckets.

"We didn't see it coming. Didn't see their fangs till they'd sunk them in. Like you. Did you learn your lesson?"

"We did," he said, "we see what they're up to. The Brits and Spaniards are always lying in wait, on the pretext of debts they imposed ages ago."

"The Brits and Spaniards . . . *and the French.*"

"No, no. Not the French; not anymore."

The man stopped what he was doing and gave him a curious look.

"Not the French."

"The French have a history of atrocities too, of course, but they've changed. France gave us the philosophy of reason. And once that takes hold, there's no turning back."

"Reason," said the man, now cutting the tail, which took noticeably more effort. "Reason isn't just a concept that comes out of books. Reason also comes in the form of firepower."

The man stopped carving a moment and laughed.

"But, hey, good luck." Setting the knife to one side, he took up the machete again, and in one clean blow amputated a gator foot and handed it to him. "Here. Something to remember me by."

In March came the epiphany of the brothel.

It wasn't far, on the last street at the edge of the old quadrant, out by where they'd lived with Thisbee, but the streetlamps were all dark now, whether out of apathy or exhausted by Carnival. The only source of light was a fire. They arrested a man there for entering the burning house to steal paintbrushes.

The brothel had stubby candles on the tables that illuminated the contours of everything around them. Games of chance in this room, dancing in that one over there, drinks in them all. Music in a few, though it could only be sensed. Chess. In one room they were playing chess.

"What on earth?" he asked the air. Pepe and Santacilia had already vanished.

"Why so surprised?" asked someone on the other side of the wick. When the man smiled, his teeth gleamed. Paul. "Don't you know about Morphy, best player in the world? He's from here. Yessir. Creole."

Paul took a sip of his drink and Yessirred once more.

"Everyone does what they can to pass the time, right? You, for example, you sniff around." He leaned in to say this, waggling the fingers of one hand as if they were sniffing. "Me, I take my medicine and make conversation; if you want to get to know folks, you've got to converse with them, cause I tell you, it's not what you know, it's *who* you know, right? *Who you know.* Incidentally, *her* I think you already know."

Paul gave him a slap on the back and disappeared in the direction of the bar. Thisbee, all business, grabbed his arm and pulled him into a room off to the side.

"Are we going to dance?" he asked in excitement.

"Not today. But the noise is good cover. I hear you've been asking around. If there's something you want to know, why don't you ask me outright."

"What does that drawing mean?"

"Exactly what it looks like: that moving forward doesn't mean you abandon what's left behind. Sankofa."

"Like what?"

"It's different for everyone. A history, a place."

"A person."

"Yes."

Thisbee looked at the dancers without seeing them.

"You're going home soon, right?"

"Yes."

"Can you find my person refuge?"

Who was this refugee to her? And where could he find them refuge?

"Yes, inasmuch as refuge is possible in a country at war, I think so, yes. Tomorrow I'll write to make some inquiries."

Thisbee nodded.

"I have to go," she said. "You stay here awhile. But first come with me. I want to show you another conspiracy."

She led him down a hall, opened the door to an inner courtyard, and gave him a gentle shove. The space was larger than others he'd seen: an orchestra played but nobody was dancing, or they were but at a low frequency, as if dancing inward. He looked to his side; she was already gone.

He approached the orchestra. Three violinists were playing a waltz. Yes, it was a waltz, no doubt about it. He'd heard it in Oaxaca, back when he was governor, but this was something else. Behind the violinists he saw the man with the very long drum: he didn't play the instrument so much as scratch at it with slack hands, almost as if by accident: a gentle stroke that turned into tapping when he switched from fingernails to fingertips, playing off the waltz without yielding to it. And the violins, despite following the beat, were also doing something different: they were having a conversation, each saying the same thing in their own pitch.

All this time the ingredients had been in front of his face, he'd simply never imagined them together. It was a miraculous invention but incomplete. Could it be completed? Or was that the miracle, that it never stopped spinning, scaling the walls?

SEVEN

A cigar is made from the inside out, as if familiar with the elements. The binder—that's the leaf that holds it together—is placed on a small table; onto the binder go the guts, which some call filler: this gives it the flavor, the scent, the burn. The cigar is rolled ever so slowly, with enough pressure to make the guts seem like one, the filler all of a piece. Then the tips are trimmed with a blade, the wrapper leaf is applied, the whole thing is smoothed and rounded, and finally on goes the little cap. The length is then measured with a triangle, the breadth with a ring gauge.

They place the cigars in a box before Borrego returns, pocketing a few as payment, which they sell to buy food and coffee.

A man named Young, sentenced to death for killing a child, attempted to commit suicide two days before his execution, stabbing himself in the stomach and slitting his own throat. Young was given just enough medical attention to make it to the scaffold alive. After seeing an ad for the execution, for whatever reason, he went off to witness it. It took some twenty minutes for Killer Young to die. In that time the gash on his throat split, his chest and trousers were soaked in blood.

This was weeks ago, but he couldn't get it out of his head, the image of a man who'd been stitched up, and then killed and killed and killed again, by the doctors, by the hangman, and by himself, he who'd watched the man bleed.

"The law is so awful," he was going to say, but Pepe got a tug on his line, and it sank down into the depths. Pepe stood up, pulled in the line, and a fish appeared, wriggling on the little hook. Perhaps it was because they so rarely caught anything, and fishing was merely an excuse to gaze at the river and pretend they were coursing along with it; or perhaps they were just hungry; but Pepe was overjoyed, and in his boyish glee he threw the fish over his shoulder, as if showing off, as if it were a shark and not some little fishie.

"The law is so awful," he was going to say, "that the only way to live with it is for it to be equally awful for all: no fueros, no privileges, no exceptions. *That* should be our point of departure."

Clip-clop-clop come the hooves of Twigs's horse; he recognizes its graceless gait, the riderless lack of rhythm. The horse walked ahead when they were on their regular route, and behind when the other animal, the one in clothes, went off course. He stops to wait for them and is reached first by the quadruped and then by the biped, at which point he asks the latter why not leave the horse in the stable if he's never going to ride it, plus why does he never ride it. The minute he asks, a grimace of pain leads him to suspect that Twigs lives in some hemorrhoidal hellscape, but the man responds in what's intended to be a hostile, dignified tone:

122

"Ride him or not, no self-respecting man goes out in the world without his horse."

Mata returned, just for a few days. He'd been in Brownsville, and then in other parts of Louisiana. In Brownsville, pursuing Josefa and hiding from Ocampo. In Louisiana, because he ran out of money and spent a few months earning his keep, teaching here and there. He returned impatient and angry, It's too much, It's disgraceful, It can't go on like this. Who knows whether *it* referred to the exile he'd grown tired of or to the new exile he'd discovered, the one far from Josefa, but the man had decided it was time to go home.

On that they agreed, though odds were they each meant something else by *go home*.

He wrote to Brownsville, to Tamaulipas, to Guerrero, to Veracruz. And everyone said yes, they'd take his man, and then everyone added various versions of But, you know, things being what they are, it's at his own risk. Veracruz and Tamaulipas already had small colonies of fugitive slaves, but right now it was impossible to disembark in Veracruz. So Tamaulipas, then. Later, if they won the war, they could move him south. And if they didn't win the war, no matter where the man was, he'd be better off than they would.

The first stretch would need to be overland: impossible to sneak a wanted man onto a ship, no matter how dead he was. People here knew about possums too.

Weeks earlier, he'd chosen the very day of his birth (also the official start of spring in places where the hot is not what structures time) to write to Brownsville that he was ready, suggesting Guerrero as his ultimate destination: that's where he'd be the most use. What he neglected to add is that it wasn't only a strategic decision but also an emotional one: he would get on better with the black rebellion in the south than with the frockcoat conspiracy at the border.

He also wondered, for the first time, what he'd take with him, whether the gator foot wouldn't be enough.

Cabañas agreed to forge the passenger's papers: what name should they put down?, he didn't know, but it had to be a Mexican name, what did that mean?, Spanish. They pondered: a common Christian name and a surname with a story. José del Río. Reference the river, not bad. Juan Veloz. Right, he was speedy. Sebastián Recio. Yep, tough as nails. Jesús Robles, strong as oak. I like it. They fell silent. Then he asked what on earth they were thinking. If there was one thing they couldn't do, it was impose a name on this man. He said he'd ask Thisbee. Oh, and also: they'd need to keep moving him from one place to another right up until they departed. Could he stay at the workshop for a spell?

"My courage only goes so far," Cabañas replied. "One day I'm going home too, and I don't want to get booted before my time."

So: a plan for the fugitive, check, or almost-check. A route for himself, check: cross the Gulf without docking in Mexican territory, on to Panama, cross the isthmus by train or wagon, board another ship in the Pacific, sail on to liberated territory, disembark in Acapulco. It would take over a month but it was the only way. The money would come: the Brownsville gang were now the Brownsville Revolutionary Junta and raising funds very efficiently. His affairs here, almost-check: all he needed was Madame Doubard and Borrego to come back so he could settle up, say thanks and so long.

Methodically, he'd always said: if you proceed methodically, things run like clockwork.

Like a furry beam of light, Polaris bounded down from upstairs a split second before the sound of a door put an end to the plotting that he, Pepe, and Thisbee had been engaged in, and there in the doorframe stood Madame Doubard, all aflutter. Polaris leapt into her arms and the two of them began spinning in circles, kissing, wagging their curls, Polaris barking, Madame Doubard repeating something, whatever it was, some syllable in the language of elation. She set Polaris on the floor and began swiveling downward, lowering her center of gravity, and Polaris followed her, jumping up on two paws; they were the loveliest dance partners he'd ever seen, one of the loveliest delights he'd ever witnessed, which he wanted to say but couldn't, because he was crying.

"I hope you haven't polished off all my booze," Madame Doubard said, finally addressing them, "cause tonight we're having the mother of all shindigs."

"Madame," said one. "Madame," replied the other. Thisbee and Madame Doubard. No need for introductions, no How do you do, no What can I offer you, no Sorry to bother you, no namby-pamby nonsense. Madame, madame, and the two of them began to drink. Pepe began to drink. Others began to

125

arrive, friends of Madame Doubard's, friends of Thisbee's, friends of Pepe's, and then he went off to get Cabañas, and everyone began to drink and to try on the clothes that were hanging on the mannequin. The two women chatted and chatted, like they'd known each other all their lives or like they'd had to know each other all their lives, and even though there was still plotting to do, he didn't want to interrupt whatever they were saying or the dance they were sharing.

It wasn't until later, when Thisbee was on her way out, that he told her where he planned to hide the man and finally asked his name.

"Is this okay?" he asked, showing the man a document that bore his names. Miguel Miguel. Two times. That was the way he'd wanted it. Miguel Miguel, the first because it was the name he went by, the second to underscore his rejection of his captor's name. They'd gone to Borrego's clinic at midnight and he'd told him to sleep on the cot, but if anyone came, to hide under a table in the backroom, where he'd hung a blanket by way of a curtain. Miguel Miguel nodded and said nothing. The man was tall, strong, and very young, despite the hundreds of years in his eyes, which glowered at the walls as if he wanted to fell them with his fists.

He had addressed Miguel Miguel in English, but it struck him the man would have understood no matter what language: he was sharp, tuned in to every detail of the situation at every second.

What could he say for himself—with no shame—about his days in this city, he'd wondered on the day he went off to obtain that girl's daguerreotype for fraud. Now he knew. He had a simple, coherent, communicable story, something to put this chapter of his life in order.

Borrego returned as well, healthy, portly, and satisfied, like an emperor back from Gaul. As soon as they saw him, he and Pepe pulled out the boxes of cigars for Borrego to count, but he barely looked at them. He set about regaling them with his plans to bring back the business; he'd learned new healing techniques involving magnets—incredible, science never stops—and made new contacts for his other lines of work; now he'd need to reestablish local contacts with the Registrars, the police. Good times on the horizon. Borrego fell silent and went into the backroom; in one quick glance he took it all in.

"Just as I remembered it," he said, and seemed to believe it.

The wooden counter was unattended; behind it hung a curtain not unlike the one at Borrego's, but this one was thick and black and velvety. He stroked it as he would an animal that might flinch on contact. Pulling the curtain aside, he caught sight of the daguerreotypist. The man's hands were up, as if framing the image before him: a family, stock-still, awaiting preservation on the silver mirror.

Something in the pallor of the photographed family made him shiver. Without thinking, he went in and stood off to one side.

It was a couple and a boy. He was white, she was black, the boy was brown. The man had been crying and the woman was dead.

The daguerreotypist lowered his hands, indicating they

127

were done, then went to the family to escort the boy out, while the man carried the woman in his arms. When the daguerreotypist turned, he saw him but said nothing and walked out with the family.

He heard them exchange a few words in the front room. He saw the collection of plates in a display case, picked up one with the image of a pretty young woman; how could he take it, with nothing to give in return? The daguerreotypist came back in and gave him an exhausted sort of attention, but then walked over and studied him with something like wonder. The daguerreotypist gestured for him to take the plate in his hands and then walked over to the chairs, removed one—the one where the man had been sitting—and gestured to the other with an open hand. Not knowing how to refuse, he merely waved his arms, but the daguerreotypist kept insisting he sit.

In the end he did not sit: he stood beside the chair, with one hand on its back. The daguerreotypist slid in a new plate, adjusted the lighting, signaled for him to stand still, and he did. He stood still and waited.

EIGHT

His body's center was shifting, as if his gravity were being trans-
ferred from his torso to his blood, making every earnest atom
inside him fall away like useless clothing, while his bonebag
took its cues from his coccyx, which was acting like the guy
who awakens mid-bender and starts shouting Hey, hey, hey,
arriba, arriba; this was his secret self, the one he let himself be
led by when dancing. It was like he got smaller and turned into
a spinning top, he who was already so stubby. He flapped his
fists as if charged with making waves in the air, took steps that
might or might not be the ones called for by protocol, what
did he care, especially here, where folks spicked-and-spanned
their sarabands and shook up their contradance with no re-
gard for the score, and especially when he was with Thisbee,
who kept saying in shock, Look at you! Look at you! He spun
circles around her, inched in like at a cockfight, backed up,
clapped, elbowed the air, shimmied his hips, lordly hips, sul-
tan of the coccyx, hey, hey, hey.

A little ways away or in up close, but never glued together:
the only woman whose waist he'd embrace was Margarita, and
hers the only hand he'd hold. Not that he didn't feel the urge:
the urge is what wore him out on the floor.

That was why he nearly soiled himself when Thisbee motioned to the orchestra, the drummer slowed his drumming, and the other musicians followed suit. Thisbee placed her hands on his shoulders and he couldn't figure out where to put his own, but then he remembered an old-time style, slipped his arms beneath hers, and brought his open hands together behind her, pinkie to pinkie; despite not touching her back, their bodies were now even closer. Thisbee said What are you doing, and he said This is called the book dance; for a second she looked stunned but then roared with laughter. Methinks you put too much faith in books; are you saying I'm easy to read? No, he replied, but I am learning a little.

He'd be gone in a few hours. They'd come to the brothel to celebrate getting everything set. First he'd taken Miguel a sack of food and water that Thisbee had given him, and to explain that in the morning they'd be borrowing a horse. As they were speaking, they heard the door, and Miguel hid under the table. It was Borrego. Since they had already said their farewells, he told Borrego he'd only come by to collect a few things and would leave the keys in a drawer. Borrego had come by for some cash. They exchanged a few final words, Borrego took his leave, and then he himself went to the bawdyhouse. Only now did it hit him, the last thing Borrego had said:

"Looks like we're not going to see each other again, since I won't be back till tomorrow or the day after. You take care now. And stop talking to yourself."

All at once he stopped dancing, cracking the spine of the book he'd been holding at Thisbee's back.

"I've got to go get Miguel. We need to move everything up."

Borrego had never told him if he was coming or going, or when.

"Go find Madame Doubard, tell her I'm bringing her another guest, though just for a minute."

More important: Borrego had heard him speaking.

Most important: no way would Borrego forfeit a reward.

He ran to the doctor's office, wondering how he'd find a horse at that hour: there was more chance of being struck by lightning.

"We're leaving. Now," he said. Miguel immediately saw that the plan had gone wrong and stood, ready to run for it, without wanting to bring a single thing. He, however, grabbed the bag of food and a metal canteen and they were off.

Hardly had they shut the door when they heard lightning strike.

"Trifling as you look, I knew one day you'd bring me something worth my while."

Twigs was speaking to him but looking at Miguel, not in triumph, more savoring his hatred, already eviscerating the man in his mind. He and Miguel froze for a moment, then he saw the horse approaching, and perhaps it was calculated or perhaps it was the revulsion Twigs's expression induced, but either way it was enough to do what had to be done: he swung the sack holding the canteen with all his might, striking Twigs in the jaw, and Twigs folded, buckling to the ground like an ox.

Miguel shot him a look of surprise; this was the first time his face had shown anything but flinty rage. He took the horse by the reins and all three of them raced to the house on Saint Peter. Quickly he explained what he feared and what he knew and what he'd done, which all amounted to the same thing as far as the upshot: Miguel had to go—now. Thisbee told Miguel to ride to Tiger Island—which wasn't an island but was called one because it was surrounded by channels and had lots of big cats—and someone would take him down the Atchafalaya to the Gulf.

Miguel made as if to mount the horse.

"Careful," he told him, "this one's not used to being ridden."

Miguel stroked the horse's mane, its head, placed his face in front of the animal's, and breathed together with it for a minute, then mounted it easily and without a fight. Once atop the horse, he put a hand in his pocket, pulled something out, and handed it to him. The compass. Somehow, Miguel had got it back. He kissed Thisbee's cheek and rode off.

"My son," she said, and he was surprised not by this revelation but by the fact that Thisbee was about to cry, since crying was something he thought she didn't do. And she didn't.

"Why doesn't your son speak?"

"He does. But he's got nothing left to say to this place."

They heard footsteps on the corner, approaching quickly, and everyone rushed inside. Soon there came a knock on the door. He, Thisbee, and Pepe slipped into a backroom and Madame Doubard went to answer. They dared not so much as sigh; even Polaris, who'd come with them, was on alert and silent.

"Yes?" came Madame Doubard's voice, betraying a twinge of kindly irritation.

"I've come for the outlaws that're hiding here," said Twigs.

For a second there was no sound; then Madame Doubard said:

"The only outlaws here are me and my dog."

As if she'd been called, Polaris bounded out to her and began to growl. He peeked out from the backroom.

"Either you bring them out or I'm going to need to come in and fetch them," Twigs said.

"Ha! Look, monsieur," she replied, now speaking majestic French, "entering a woman's house unbidden at this hour would be the least of your concerns. The greatest one, the truly grave one, would be what *this* woman, so accustomed to living alone, might do to an intruder."

Coolly, she took a candelabra from the entry table and held it one-handed, as if testing its weight.

Though they were the ones in the backroom, at that moment Madame Doubard *was* the backroom, the site of conspiracy personified.

"I'll be back," Twigs said, "with officers, with cuffs."

"We'll be waiting. And don't forget your horse," replied Madame Doubard, in English now, "but do something about that hangover first. You're looking a bit liverish."

And with that she closed the door. Then did a little celebratory jig.

"I have one last favor to ask," he said.

She said yes, said of course.

They could no longer take luggage. He removed the gator foot from his case and hung it from his belt. Then he picked up one end of Madame's mannequin while Pepe picked up the other. They'd go to the levee together but board different ships, and Pepe would try to return to Oaxaca.

He hated goodbyes, because he found it impossible to be fittingly dramatic or suitably verbose: farewell speeches are always insufficient. But also because goodbyes are a time when both the situation being left behind and the one about to begin totter precariously on the edge of a table. He gave her a hug, and Madame Doubard said If you decide to come back and rope me into your criminality again, kindly brief me in advance; I'd do it all over, of course, but preferably without the heart attack.

He embraced Polaris, who began chewing on their shoes, as if to leave him and Pepe no means of departure; Polaris, she knew how to say a proper goodbye. Then he turned to Thisbee and she hugged him so hard and so long he thought he'd come to pieces.

"Teach them what it means to have music inside you."

He and Pepe went back to Borrego's. They stuck the mannequin in the backroom and doused it in alcohol. He lit a match, but then stopped.

"What are you doing?" asked Pepe. "We have to go."

Borrego was a bastard, but the man had given them food to eat and a cure, the kind that worked. And what had he done in exchange? Hidden in the backroom the man who murdered his friend. Perhaps Borrego's understanding of *friend* was questionable, but the man didn't deserve to have his office torched in order to cover a killer's tracks.

"Let's get out of here," he said. "I mean, how many times does Miguel have to die before they stop chasing him, anyway? Miguel's gone and they don't know where; he's got the upper hand."

Pepe snorted. He blew out the match, put it back in his jacket, and left the keys where he'd promised. They began walking to the dock, calm but on the qui vive, like cats crossing the street; before they'd even made it a block, a burst of flame came from behind them. They turned and saw Borrego's office start to burn. And then Borrego, emerging from the flames, dragging a box. The two of them ran back to help; once they were all safe from the fire, Borrego said:

"I don't understand; why didn't you go through with it? You had the right idea. When I saw you change your mind, I decided to do it myself. All you need to get the reward is a body, or something resembling one, and a good story, which is the kind I tell; I have a certain credibility with the authorities, you see . . . As for the rest of it"—he pointed to the office engulfed in flames—"the insurance business is like a sport here, you know. The authorities will be good for that, at least. They're on their way now."

Borrego wasn't giving them a warning; he was making calculations. All three of them stood for a few minutes, entranced by the flames. Then Pepe tugged on his arm and they began walking away without saying goodbye.

Then they ran, but after a few blocks he said:

"Wait, slow down; we have time."

And they did—not much, but that wasn't it. What he wanted was to feel the city one last time. It struck him that if one day he was dropped there without anyone telling him where he was, he'd know it was New Orleans even with his eyes closed. He couldn't explain it. It was just that in his bones he'd be able to feel the shifting ground beneath the cobbles, resisting. And that he didn't actually have his story straight; that there was no simple, coherent, communicable tale to tell; that there were too many betrayals, small ones or secret ones but betrayals nonetheless; and that he had a right to keep them to himself, in all the tongues he now knew. Then he said:

"Okay. Now we run."

They arrived moments before Pepe's steamer set sail.

"Look after those letters, and look after my family," he pleaded. "I'll be back sooner rather than later."

Pepe, a little teary, nodded and boarded the ship so as not to show it.

At the foot of the gangway to his own steamboat, Santacilia was waiting for him.

"When will we see each other again?" Santacilia asked.

"Fuck knows."

Santacilia laughed.

"I don't know how that'll sound when the time comes for me to tell the tale. We'll see what I can come up with."

The two men shook hands. Finally, the last goodbye. He turned and walked up the gangway; a ticket-taker asked his name.

"Benito Juárez García," he replied.

He entered the passengers' cabin. The day's papers were already there. As the boat weighed anchor, he began leafing through them. The allies and the Russians were still killing one other in Crimea; in a recent battle, eight thousand men had died in a single night, almost all by bayonet. A bookstore on Camp Street announced the arrival of new books. A group of men, armed with machetes, had made a jailbreak. The Pelican was showing a comedy that night: *The Jacobite*, a benefit for the widow of one of the actors. High temperatures had caused several people to collapse on the street: summer was back.

The ship began to move.

He put down the paper and went out to stand on deck, and saw that the fire was burning furiously. He walked out to the prow, leaned over the railing, and began to look forward, at the way home, illuminated by the glow behind.

ACKNOWLEDGMENTS

Thanks go to Juan Álvarez, Brenda Navarro, and Fernando Rivera, for their readings and advice.

To Robert Ticknor, of the Historic New Orleans Collection, for his invaluable research support.

To Paca Flores and Julián Rodríguez, for all the years of generous, intelligent company.

Yuri Herrera was born in Actopan, Mexico, in 1970 and is the author of the novels *Kingdom Cons, Signs Preceding the End of the World,* and *The Transmigration of Bodies,* which have been translated into many languages. He is also the author of the story collections *Ten Planets* and *Talud,* and of the nonfiction book *A Silent Fury: The El Bordo Mine Fire.* In 2016 he shared with translator Lisa Dillman the Best Translated Book Award for *Signs Preceding the End of the World.* That same year he was also awarded the Anna Seghers Prize at the Academy of Arts of Berlin. He is a professor of creative writing and literature at Tulane University in New Orleans.

Lisa Dillman is a translator from Los Angeles and lives in Atlanta. She has translated more than thirty novels into English, including all of Yuri Herrera's books available in English (*Ten Planets, Kingdom Cons, Signs Preceding the End of the World,* which won the Best Translated Book Award, *The Transmigration of Bodies,* and *A Silent Fury: The El Bordo Mine Fire*). Other writers she has translated include Pilar Quintana, Alejandra Costamagna, and Graciela Mochkovsky. Her translations of Pilar Quintana's *The Abyss* and *The Bitch* were both finalists for the National Book Award for Translated Literature. She teaches in the Department of Spanish and Portuguese at Emory University.

Graywolf Press publishes risk-taking, visionary writers who transform culture through literature. As a nonprofit organization, Graywolf relies on the generous support of its donors to bring books like this one into the world.

This publication is made possible, in part, by the voters of Minnesota through a Minnesota State Arts Board Operating Support grant, thanks to a legislative appropriation from the arts and cultural heritage fund. Significant support has also been provided by other generous contributions from foundations, corporations, and individuals. To these supporters we offer our heartfelt thanks.

MINNESOTA
STATE ARTS BOARD

CLEAN
WATER
LAND &
LEGACY
AMENDMENT

To learn more about Graywolf's books
and authors or make a tax-deductible donation,
please visit www.graywolfpress.org.

The text of *Season of the Swamp* is set in Ten Oldstyle Medium. Book design and composition by Bookmobile Design & Digital Publisher Services, Minneapolis, Minnesota. Manufactured by Friesens on acid-free, 100 percent postconsumer wastepaper.